# *Ghosts* LIVE HERE

## C.C. BROWN

## About the Authors

CC Brown is the pseudonym adopted by two sisters, Schyrlet Cameron and Kathy Brown. Growing up in the Ozarks, their curiosity about the supernatural was sparked by their grandmother. As children, much of their time was spent on their grandparents' farm, where their grandmother always kept them entertained… tending the garden, feeding the chickens, milking the cows, and telling deliciously spooky late-night tales. Their fascination with ghosts and spirits from beyond the grave has not diminished over time.

# Most Haunted Hotel in America
## Eureka Springs, Arkansas

The story of the Crescent Hotel is linked to the history of Eureka Springs, Arkansas—they both exist because of the local water. Thousands were drawn to the town because of the "healing waters" that reportedly bubbled up from the more than sixty springs in and around the downtown area. According to historians, the springs were originally discovered by the Osage in the early 1800s. The tribe would bathe in the waters, saying it contained healing spirits.

After the native Americans were forced out of the area years later, the waters were rediscovered. Around 1850, Dr. Alva Jackson stumbled upon the springs with his son. It is reported the doctor's son had an eye irritation. Dr. Jackson used the water from the springs as a cure.

The Crescent Hotel opened its doors in

1886. She was considered by many to be the crowning jewel of the Ozarks. The resort was built by the Eureka Springs Improvement Company and the Frisco Railroad as a way to take advantage of tourists who flocked to the Ozark region for its natural springs. The massive limestone structure was reminiscent of the castles of Europe. Stonemasons brought from Ireland helped construct the five-story fortress. An exclusive hot spot for the elite, the inside was elegantly furnished. Outside, a park surrounded the hotel with tennis courts and gardens.

From 1908 to 1923 and again from 1929 to1933, the building severed two purposes. Due to slow business in the winter months, the hotel operated as the Crescent College and Conservatory for young women. Summer months, it severed as a popular getaway for the elite. The "Grand Ol' Lady of The Ozarks" closed her doors in 1934 at the height of the Great Depression because few had the money for higher education or summer resorts.

In 1937, Norman G. Baker purchased the property. Baker converted the hotel into a cancer hospital and treated hundreds of patients. He liked to refer to the Crescent as the "Castle in the Air." In 1940, Baker was jailed for mail fraud and the hospital closed.

In 1946, four businessmen from Chicago—Herbert A. Byfield, John R Constantine, Dwight O. Nichols, and Herbert E. Shutter—bought and refurbished the Crescent. The new owners worked with the Frisco Railroad, offering travel vacation packages to bring new tourists to the area. In 1967, a fire destroyed most of the fourth floor and heavily damaged the third level. The Crescent again, sat abandoned. In 1972, a partnership bought the hotel, rescuing it from being turned into a chicken farm. After major construction and refurbishment, the Crescent re-opened in 1973.

The present owners, Marty and Elise Roenigk, purchased the Crescent in 1997 and began renovations to the hotel and grounds that restored the property to its former glory. The Roenigks renamed the resort the "1886 Crescent Hotel & Spa." In 2007, the U.S. Department of the Interior listed the 1886 Crescent Hotel & Spa on the National Register of Historic Places.

Rumors, questions, and theories have swirled around the castle on the mountaintop for decades. One such rumor claimed there was something special about the place that made guests imagine the halls and rooms were inhabited with ghosts, poltergeists, and other supernatural beings. Others declared it an eerily spooky place with unexplained occurrences that needed to be studied, verified, and documented for future generations.

*Ghosts Live Here* was inspired by the mysterious and unexplainable events we, personally, experienced during our many stays at the Crescent Hotel. In writing our story, we tried to stay true to the history of the area and the historic hotel. We focused on facts and true incidents that have occurred. While, in several instances, the actual names and locations of people and businesses have been used, the facts surrounding the actual people and occurrences have been embellished. We personally look forward to revisiting the town of the "healing waters" and the historic hotel to further investigate the spirits of the paranormal kind.

# 1886 Cresent Hotel and Spa

Courtesy of Eureka Springs Historical Museum

# Ghosts Live Here

The boundaries which divide Life from Death are at best shadowy and vague. Who shall say where the one ends, and where the other begins?

-Edgar Allan Poe,<br>"The Premature Burial"

## Prologue
## Eureka Springs, Arkansas

**Darkness** fell like the thick velvet stage curtains of a medieval theater. It was as if the daytime had been Act One of a play. There was no light left save that of the stars. A sliver of moon rose over the horizon signaling Act Two was about to begin.

Low-lying mist covered the thick forest of pine trees and firs. Above the fog, the magnificent century-old castle rose into the night sky atop the highest point of the mountain. Worthy of its very own Grimms' Fairy Tale, the massive stone structure towered above the sleepy Victorian village like some ancient fortress overlooking its kingdom.

The castle walls were the strongest structure for miles around. It was built of limestone blocks in varying sizes and shapes, each one unique. From a distance, it was uniform gray; from up close, it was a

1

mosaic of humble stone blocks, each of them something no one would think anything if found loose by the roadside. But, together, they were a grand palace.

The landmark was steeped in history and tradition. It had stood the test of time, surviving wars, fires, and economic chaos. Decades old, the castle had many lives: hotel, college, and hospital. But, in between, there had been years when the fortress sat vacant and uncared for. It stood neglected, silent. Absent of love, it grew lonely... a loneliness beyond endurance.

Within the castle, the great hearth turned dark and cold; secret places were forgotten. Sunshine and the warm winds of summer only raised sad memories of a time when the castle had been loved and cherished. The only friends—true old friends—were the ones who had come to stay and never left. Yet, they scarcely warded off the loneliness.

For years, the beautiful old estate sat, rotting. Once a glorious Victorian retreat full of life and laughter, it now rested solemnly in the shadows. It began to fear its fate, an eternity on its own. The countless lonely years began to take its toll, and, gradually, the castle changed.

It began as small random acts: creaking stairs… shifting shadows… whispering voices. Yet, as with any journey, those small steps became more significant and ominous as they added up. Over time, the castle's soul turned to the dark side. It felt no compassion… no remorse… no fear. After all, what was there to be afraid of when it was now the monster?

# Chapter 1

**A** hint of pumpkin spice and apple pie floated on the crisp evening air. Nicole locked the door to Main Street Mercantile and headed for the pie shop next door when someone called her name. Turning, she saw a red Chrysler pull up. She walked over and peeked inside.

The van door slid open, and, to Nicole's surprise, someone grabbed her from behind. She went to scream when the person whispered, "Did I scare you?" then shoved her inside.

*Oh my God, I'm being kidnapped!* As the Chrysler pulled away from the curb and sped down the deserted street, unable to put voice to her thoughts, she could only wonder, *What's this world coming to? One minute you're on your way home to a cozy fire and a good book, and the next, you find yourself in the back of a speeding van… destination unknown.*

Nicole knew the first few minutes of abduction were the riskiest, and, to survive, she would have to rely on all her skills and wits. She decided the best line of defense was to cooperate and empathize with the two captors: her sister and her best friend.

Gathering blonde strands and pulling them through a hair tie from her wrist, Nicole said to the back of her sister's head, "I didn't expect to get kidnapped today or I would have worn something more appropriate."

Turning in the seat, eyebrows raised, Kat cautioned, "Remember what Mom always said…"

Sapphire-blue eyes glaring, Nicole held up her hand, "Don't you dare go there! I'm in no mood for one of your *Rules Our Southern Parents Taught Us*."

Ignoring the warning, Kat continued with a smirk, "Some rules are made to be broken. And then there are the rules our mom taught us that we should never disobey. Rule # 25: Always put on clean underwear before leaving the house."

"I'm finding it really hard to see any humor in this abduction scheme of yours, Kat!"

Her best friend, Mariah, intervened while

signaling and switching lanes, "Sit back and enjoy the ride. If done right, kidnapping can be a positive experience for everyone."

"And who did you steal that line from?" Nicole questioned, frowning at the back of the getaway driver's head.

"Jim Carrey," Mariah replied, getting a belly chuckle from Kat.

"You should be thanking us," Kat insisted.

"And why is that?"

"We could have thrown a burlap bag over your head and zip-tied your hands," Kat answered, sending Mariah into a fit of laughter.

"God help me, I've been kidnaped by a couple of would-be comedians," Nicole spit out, thoroughly disgusted. "Why all the secrecy, Kat?" Nicole asked, not expecting her sister to give her a straight answer, but, as an eternal optimist, she could only hope for the truth.

Checking the mirror for traffic, Mariah answered for Kat. "This is Fall Festival weekend, so we have planned a special treat."

"Yah, so sit back, take in the fall foliage, and leave the driving to us. We're going to have a great time," Kat declared with a big smile meant to reassure the victim.

Remembering the disastrous weekend getaway Kat had arranged last summer, she had her doubts. In Nicole's opinion, a spooky hotel with haunted halls and ghosts around every corner did not make for a relaxing retreat. So, based on her sister's track record, Nicole interpreted the cryptic clues as: Fall Festival = Halloween Fright Night. Special treat = two days of hell with the undead.

Nicole glanced from the driver to the front seat passenger. *Oh, they are definitely up to something.* Knowing the two in the front weren't about to slip up and reveal any of the essential details of their plot, Nicole sat back and turned her attention to the passing scenery. The thick hardwood forests of the Ozark Mountains glowed vivid shades of orange, red, and yellow in the setting sunlight. Soon, all thoughts of spooky hotels and monsters in the night were lost in the beauty of the fall colors and the changing leaves. The soft, rocking motion of the car, along with the purr of the engine, soon lulled her to sleep.

Meanwhile, the co-conspirators plotted as the van climbed the steep winding highway. "The fight will be on when she figures out where we're headed," Mariah warned, finger-combing a wild tangle of dark curls back into the braid over her shoulder.

Watching the sun sink lower behind the mountains, Kat said, "It'll be too late then." She felt a strange chill, and her eyes were drawn to the roadside. A feeling of loneliness filled her as several white wooden crosses, marking a makeshift memorial, swept by.

Shaking off the feeling, she pulled her sweater closer. "This is for her own good," Kat defended her decision while silently hoping she was doing the right thing.

"Nicole is stuck in the past. There's no scientific proof of an afterlife or spirits, and, yet, she is convinced that what happened last year at the 1905 Basin Park Hotel was real," Kat explained, astounded at her sister's wrongheaded thinking… but, although she would never admit it, the late summer stay in Eureka Springs had unnerved her, too. Now a reformed paranormal denier, she considered herself a part-time believer. During the day, she didn't believe in ghosts, but, at night, she was a little more open-minded and more determined than ever to find a scientific explanation.

The van continued climbing. Daylight gave way to the evening shadows as the road cut through the woods. Soon, the three travelers were hemmed in by trees. The branches crashed together as the women swept along. A dog began to howl somewhere far down the highway. Another dog took up the sound, and then another and another. Their mournful cries echoed over the dark hills and through the lonely hollows of the forest. Kat felt uncertain and a little frightened as she listened to the mournful music they made.

In time, the sorrowful baying of the hounds grew fainter as Mariah navigated the serpentine road, climbing higher and higher. She kept a watchful eye on the shadows within the shadows of the forest as they approached the sleeping village. A quick glance at the car's dashboard clock gave her a shock. It was within a few minutes of midnight. Her granny always claimed, "The midnight hour is the time of night when the veil between life and death is thinnest, allowing spirits and ghosts to travel between the two worlds."

Nicole awoke to the van weaving a path along a narrow, winding mountain street lined with Victorian homes hugging steep cliffs. A thick row of trees on both sides formed a canopy. The moonlight filtered through the leaf-covered branches, casting ominous shadows, adding a dark foreboding feel to the ride. She waited with a sick feeling of suspense. *I know this place*.

The van rounded a curve and turned onto Prospect Avenue. Time seemed endless as the car slow-rolled the last few feet of the avenue, showcasing the spectacular beauty of the resort.

Beyond the torchlight of the sculptured gardens, the magnificent hotel rose into the night sky atop the highest point of the mountain. The massive five-story limestone structure towered above Eureka Springs, Arkansas, like some ancient, royal European castle.

The van came to a stop in front of the hotel. Mariah quickly opened the car's sliding doors, signaling the porter to assist her with the luggage. The bulging suitcases were unloaded onto a cart while the other two passengers stepped to the red carpet.

Kat walked up the steps to the entrance, but Nicole stood in silence where she was. She did not know what to do. For her, this Ozark Mountain town was the stuff night-mares were made of.

A stray gust of wind drifted down the empty drive, waking a momentary rustling of trees at her back. Leaves scurried along the path, and the breeze became sharper, raising goosebumps on her arms.

## Chapter 2

**The** landscape lighting cast shadowy shapes on the surrounding surfaces as the three climbed the front steps. The clock seemed to slow with each footstep until they walked through the doors into the hundred-year-old castle in the wilderness. As if propelled by an invisible hand, the enormous wood-and-glass doors slammed behind them with a roar, echoing through the corridors and dark passages.

The doorman greeted the trio, "Welcome to Eureka Springs, Arkansas, and to the 1886 Crescent Hotel and Spa, America's most haunted hotel."

For the first time, Mariah felt doubts and a little prick of fear crowding in on her. Was revisiting the town a wise decision? *Too late now*, she silently scolded herself while digging for the buckeye buried deep in her pant pocket. The power of the odd-shaped, brown nut wasn't scientific. Just like a rabbit's foot, horseshoe, or four-leaf clover, the buckeye had its doubters, but, to her, it was comforting to roll the talisman between her fingers.

With a backward glance at the moonlit courtyard, she followed Kat and Nicole into the grand foyer. The same elegance enjoyed by those at the Crescent a century ago greeted them. The tiny sparkles cast by hundreds of crystals dangling from the chandelier waltzed through the room to the strains of an imaginary orchestra. Gleaming hardwood floors, plush carpeting, and authentic Victorian furniture completed the picture.

Knowing from experience more than one person handling room reservations often needlessly complicated an otherwise straightforward and seamless process, Kat steered her sister and friend in a different direction. "You two hang around in the lobby while I get our room keys."

Thinking this was as good a time as any to confront her sister, Nicole said, "So, one haunted vacation in Eureka Springs was not enough. Oh no, you had to try it again. Honestly, Kat, I'm beginning to think there is something seriously wrong with you. On the edge of losing her temper, Nicole stopped.

Catching sight of the corner gift shop, she turned and stomped away. "I'm going to need a book."

"Well, that went better than I expected," Kat admitted to Mariah.

"Yep, consider yourself lucky. She could have pulled your hair and kicked you in the shins." Not wanting to get involved in a family feud this early in the game, Mariah said, "I'll just wait over here." With a wave, she drifted toward the center of the rotunda and settled into one of the large comfortable armchairs stationed around the open fireplace. She felt the warmth of the amber glow comforting. At times, sparks danced and leaped as if they wanted to escape and land where they may. The peaceful atmosphere provided a calming respite. An old saying came to mind, "Don't trouble trouble until trouble troubles you." Deciding the bit of folk wisdom was a good truth to live by, she put concerns about the hotel out of her mind.

As she stretched, relaxing tight shoulder muscles, her attention was drawn from the fire to a yellow tabby cat sitting in the shadows. Almost invisible, it trained an unblinking stare on her. The pupils, narrow slits, widened into black pools.

Now living on the family farm, Mariah afforded these furry creatures the respect they deserved. If you were lucky enough to own a farm in southwest Missouri, odds were good you had barn cats, whether you planned to have them or not. Most farmers in her area had a strict set of rules when it came to cats. They were not pets. You didn't get vaccines for cats or get them spayed or neutered. They had one job, pest control, and, like the alpha predators of the forest, barn cats were the farmer's most efficient killing machine.

According to last count, she had fifteen on rat patrol, a mixed breed of strays and feral cats that had decided to linger. She was quick to learn that nobody truly owned a barn cat. Most, abandoned or born in the wild with little to no human interaction, remained aloof. Even with years of feeding and living in the barn, most didn't want to be handled or touched. Many disappeared within a few months of taking up residence. One of the feral cats had given birth in the middle of the barn and then run away, never to return, so Mariah raised those five kittens on goat milk. Two had become permanent barn cats; the other three had moved on.

At first, she'd found it hard to read these secretive animals. During her daily chores, she'd studied their behavior, including body language. Over time, she'd learned that, even though they each had unique personalities and characteristics, her adopted pest control team all shared one behavior: they communicated through their eyes.

Staring back at the yellow eyes watching her, Mariah wondered aloud, "What are you trying to tell me with that feline, trance-like gaze?"

With a twitch of small, triangular ears and a flick of tail, the tabby stepped from the shadows. Like a panther in slow motion, padded paws silent, he crossed the lobby to a miniature set of carpeted steps ending at a "kitty door" to the outdoors. Once at the top, he stopped, turned, and looked directly at Mariah.

"Okay, so this is how it's going to be?" she whispered back, jumping up to follow.

But before she had taken one step, the image began to fade and, within a few seconds, disappeared.

Bewildered, Mariah did a 360-degree circle of the rotunda before her eyes landed on an oval framed photograph of a tabby cat sitting on its haunches.

She stepped closer and read, "In Memory of Morris, the Resident Cat at the Crescent Hotel."

Mariah recognized the encounter as a not-so-subtle warning from her new furry friend, "Be careful, be very careful… the dead live here." Mariah was no stranger to the paranormal, but this was the first ghost with paws she had ever encountered. In fact, she had always been able to see, feel, and communicate with "earthbound spirits," as her grandmother, with whom she shared this anomaly, called them.

Her grandma was a very talented woman: a seer of visions, finder of lost articles, community fortune-teller. She didn't advertise her special ability, but neighbors and family often stopped by for what Grandma called a "visit." Many times, as a young girl, Mariah had been directed to sit quietly and play with her dolls when company had come "calling." Guests had been ushered to the kitchen table. Cups and saucers had been taken from the pantry. Grandma had spooned a teaspoon of dark loose tea leaves into each cup, and then hot water from the kettle heating on the wood stove was poured over the leaves, filling each cup. Sipping the brew, conversation had centered on the weather, crops, and family.

Watchful, Mariah had noticed how Grandma used this time to study the person across from her. When there'd been just a sip or two of liquid left in their cup, she would place a clean cotton dishtowel on the saucer and flip the cup over to allow the excess liquid and tea leaves to drain onto the towel. Next, she'd slowly and carefully turned the cup upright and returned it to the saucer. Turning to her visitor, Grandma would caution, "The future is not fixed. Choices you make in the present can change everything." Then, peering into the cup, she'd let the tea leaves tell their story.

Unlike her grandmother, Mariah kept the inherited talent of connecting with spirits a secret while trying to live as normal a life as possible. But the ghosts would not cooperate, and it was getting harder and harder to hide the gift—or curse—from her two friends.

# Chapter 3

**Nicole** was drawn to the wall display featuring a selection of local authors. She loved books. Forget the smell of warm baked bread or freshly cleaned laundry; new or old, for her nothing compared to the smell of books. Nicole inhaled deeply. Just one whiff put her in her happy place.

To Nicole, reading was a great way to escape. It was probably the only thing that had saved her from losing her mind after the disastrous events of the last year—the death of her two-year-old son and the collapse of her marriage that had followed. Opening a chapter and reading from sentence to sentence was a cheap form of therapy. With a book in front of her nose, she could ignore the chaos of her world for just a few moments, for several hours, or an entire day. Books, to her, were treasures filled with people she would never meet and adventures she would never be brave enough to have.

Nicole credited her mother for cultivating a love of reading. At age six, she'd been taken to the library to get her own identification card. Nicole still remembered the thrill of excitement when signing the back. She'd been so proud and had immediately started imagining all the possibilities of having that little piece of paper tucked in her purse. She'd cherished that card and, to this day, kept it in her wallet as a keepsake of that special moment.

After, she'd visited the red brick building often. Sitting cross-legged for hours on the floor, surrounded by a pile of picture books she had pulled from the shelves, she'd read each one through to the end. When finished, the librarian had helped carry the books to the desk so she could checkout, and take them home to read again.

She'd quickly moved from picture books to Nancy Drew mysteries and then, as a teen, to romance novels. Now, she enjoyed all genres, occasionally reading books recommended by friends, but, for the most part, she decided what to read. And, almost entirely by accident, in that strange place between curiosity and happenstance, she always came across the right book. A story that helped her work through a problem she was struggling with.

Nicole circled the odd shaped concierge's desk to the display case filled with books. She walked along the wooden shelves crowded with dazzling debut novels, trailblazing memoirs, and inspiring historical fictional accounts of Eureka Springs and the Crescent Hotel. She ran her fingers lightly over their spines, stopping now and then to read a title, searching for just the right one. The search ended with the next book. The black-bound volume inched its way ever so slowly froward, then tumbled off the shelf, landing with a dull *thud* next to her foot. Her childhood librarian, Mrs. Duvall, had been right: "You don't choose a book, the book chooses you."

Nicole picked it up. There was some-thing deeply intimate about the book nestled in her hands. Opening the first chapter, she started reading. The feel of paper, the sound of pages turning, the beauty of the print on the paper, all gave her a strange sense of pleasure.

She remembered her mother's whispered

words, "Sometimes a book comes into your life at just the right moment." Nicole closed the black cover and read the title, *House of a Hundred Rooms* by Keith J. Scales, Tour Director at the 1886 Crescent Hotel.

# Chapter 4

**During** the day, the central hub of the resort—the lobby— buzzed with guests coming and going. Now, after midnight, it was void of activity and strangely quiet. The grand space of the entrance was inviting. French doors, wooden columns, and crimson walls promised a relaxing and enjoyable experience. Kat felt the stress of the day begin to evaporate.

Deserted by her traveling companions, Kat took a few moments to make sure she knew where to find the two after checking in. Since Nicole had been a bookworm all her life, Kat was not surprised to find her sister at the gift shop. No doubt, she would try to smuggle a packed bag to the room, intending to spend the entire weekend reading. *Wrong!* Kat had no intention of letting her sister bury herself in the world of words this trip. She had plans, and none of them included books.

It didn't take long to locate Mariah curled

up in a large, oversized chair in front of the white brick fireplace. Roommates in college, they'd become best friends—the type of friends that were always quick to point out when the other was being an ass.

Even though they had chosen different career paths, they'd remained close after graduating. Mariah had majored in farm management, while Kat, with a thirst for why and how things were the way they were, had followed her passion and gotten a degree in science education.

After graduation, they'd moved out on their own but had remained close. Kat was the one Mariah called for a ride from her ex's after trashing his apartment, and Mariah had been Kat's stability during her first year of teaching.

There were so many things that just weren't covered in the teacher education programs, and it was nearly impossible to keep up with everything on her to-do list. She didn't get much sleep, and, when she did, it would be interrupted by bad dreams and anxiety about the classroom. Chatting, venting, and laughing with Mariah over drinks got her through the rough spots.

Noticing the restless bellhop stationed

by her luggage cart, Kat headed to the reception counter. The dark-framed, wooden panels of frosted glass reminded her of a turn-of-the-century bank teller station.

Behind the glass, the clerk greeted the new arrival. She recited the hotel amenities while Kat completed the required forms. "The hotel offers breakfast in the Crystal Dining Room and pizza and drinks in the Sky Bar. There is an outdoor pool, and the spa offers a variety of services."

Kat listened politely, but already knew what the resort had to offer guests. She had done the research. The glowing customer reviews suggested the hotel had everything a guest could wish for in a luxury resort but… was it really haunted? From the online testimonials, hundreds of people believed it was. She was curious about knowing the unknown; she saw it as a game. There was only one way to find out for sure—to book a stay!

The clerk retrieved three gold keys from the network of wooden cubbies behind the desk. Pushing them forward, she said, "You're in room 419: spacious, nonsmoking, one queen and a rollaway. Is that suitable?"

Kat nodded. "Yes, it sounds like everything I expected."

"Enjoy your stay at the Crescent," the clerk said, adding the reservation to the day's paperwork arranged in neat rows on the countertop. Looking up, she finished with, "If you need anything, just dial zero on the room phone."

The hotel stirred. Old powers awakened. It had dealt with many skeptics over the years, and, as with all things that felt the need to be scary, The Grand Ol' Lady of the Ozarks was ready to play. It breathed deep and long, and, without warning, the French doors on the east side of the lobby flew open. A blast of cold wind swept through the entrance, blowing Kat's dress up to an un-lady-like height.

Like the iconic image of Marilyn Monroe posing over an updraft of a New York subway grate, Kat caught the white skirt before it blew over her head.

The gust continued wreaking havoc as it sped across the registration desk—scattering papers before it rushed out the west side double doors into the night.

In the silence which followed the flurry, Kat smoothed her chin-length, auburn bob. She fidgeted with the black-framed designer glasses. Pushing them back in place, she stared wide-eyed and opened-mouthed as the bellhop as Nicole, and Mariah scrambled to recover the papers.

Acknowledging the hotel's challenge, Kat smiled and whispered, "Bring it on!"

# Chapter 5

**Standing** in front of the grand staircase with her two friends, waiting for the elevator, Mariah hesitated. If she looked up, would she find a ghostly apparition staring down?

Not chancing it, she trained her eyes on the back of Kat's reddish-brown head and entered the giant-sized jewelry box.

The golden metal doors slid closed, and the bellhop tapped the fourth-floor button. Nicole's troubled reflection looked back at her from the mirror-like gold paneled walls. For just a tiny moment, a heartbeat long, there was something more… images, three or four with haunting faces; the rest were less clear. *Look long enough in a mirror, and one thing is sure; you'll always find something you don't like.* On her list of things she didn't like… the dead.

Turning away from the illusion, Mariah noticed the white-knuckled grip Nicole had on the golden handrails and she asked, "Is something wrong?"

"I hate elevators," Nicole explained, relaxing the death hold. She only used them if she had to, but, unfortunately, today, she really had no choice. She didn't want to be difficult, so she decided not to make a fuss.

"What?" Kat asked, not believing her ears.

"I said, I hate elevators."

Kat threw up her hands in frustration and shot Nicole a disappointed glance. "I thought you'd be over your elevator phobia by now. Let's see, how old are you… ten going on twenty-five?"

The bellhop stifled a chuckle as the elevator clanked and crept upward. Skipping the first three floors until stopping at the fourth, the doors slowly opened, revealing a long, shadowy hallway. The bellhop led the way, halting at room 419.

"You're in Theodora's room," he said, unlocking and opening the door.

"Who's Theodora?" Nicole asked.

"Are you going on the ghost tour?" the young man answered with a question.

"Yes," Kat replied before her sister could say no.

"You'll hear all about her then. You're in the second most-requested room. The tour starts outside your door."

"And this is why I travel with my own tequila," Kat announced. "You never know when you'll be stuck in a haunted hotel at midnight with a closed bar."

Luggage cart in tow, the young man entered the suite behind the guests. While unloading the luggage, he gave his practiced spiel about the hotel and local tourist attractions.

Kat stood and listened, hoping to get some useful information.

Nicole drew back the heavy curtains, revealing a spectacular view of the hotel grounds and beyond the Ozark Mountains. Nicole placed her purse and gift shop bag on the coffee table in the center of the room. Kicking off shoes, she settled on the red-velvet Victorian loveseat and immediately began rummaging for her new treasure. Hoping to discover some undeniable truth to place in her arsenal of facts about the hotel and the spirit world, she scanned the pages.

Before collecting his tip from Kat, the young man checked the lights and ensured everything was in order. Opening the door to leave, he hesitated. Turning, the hint of a smile tugging at the corners of his mouth, he said, "There's a portrait of Theodora in the master suite." And, with the announcement, he closed the door.

Locking eyes with her friends, Mariah suggested, "Let's have a look."

With a nod, Nicole tossed the book. The *thud* of the hardback landing caught Kat's attention as she knew it would.

Well aware of Nicole's passive-aggress-ive tendencies—repeatedly claiming that she was not mad or that she was fine even when she was obviously furious and not okay—Kat read the title as her sister intended. She had to smile at Nicole's clever message, *A Well-Read Woman is a Very Dangerous Adversary.*

Standing in front of the oval-framed photograph, the three studied the dark-haired woman. Mona Lisa eyes gave the uncanny feeling of being watched. It was unsettling the way they appeared to follow Nicole as she hurriedly left the room.

Returning, she quickly threw a bath towel over the oval frame. *If poets are to be believed, eyes are the windows to the soul, and I don't like what is staring back at me.* she admitted to herself.

"Hey, why are you covering it up?" Kat

insisted, watching her sister's frantic attempt to hide all traces of the wall hanging.

"I read somewhere that, sometimes, souls linger in mirrors and portraits after death."

Mariah teased, "Well, it's only fair if you think about it. We were staring at her; why shouldn't she get to stare back at us?"

Kat turned on her friend. "Shut up, Mariah." Then she tried to explain to Nicole,

"It's just an illusion. The woman is *not* watching us. It has to do with the way the painting was created."

Seeing her explanation had no effect whatsoever on Nicole, she gave up. Tomorrow was another day; she may have lost the battle over the portrait but was confident she would win the ghost wars in the end.

# Chapter 6

**The** three roommates got ready for bed in silence until Nicole asked, "Why this hotel?"

Desperate for an ally, Kat locked eyes with Mariah.

Mariah, miffed because she had to sleep on the rollaway, just flashed a knowing smile and waited. Nicole was a master interrogator; Kat didn't have a chance.

"Uh… Well…," Kat started, then stopped.

"Come on Kat, spit it out. Why *this* hotel?"

Cornered and with nowhere to run, Kat crossed her arms and said, "Okay, okay. I got an email from the Crescent promoting Eureka Springs and the annual Fall Festival. I couldn't resist the fantastic 'Spirits of the Crescent' package deal: special room rates, hatchet throwing at the Frisco Sporting Club and Pool area, relaxing at the New Moon Spa, wine tasting on the balcony of the SkyBar, and something I know you will really enjoy— s'mores at the late-night campfire."

Nicole threw up a hand in front of Kat's face, signaling, *Stop talking.* Then, letting out an exaggerated sigh, Nicole reminded Kat, "Oh, what a tangled web we weave when first we practice to deceive."

Feeling like a rat in a trap, Kat warned, "Okay, you caught me, but remember, even a trapped rat can bite."

Not in the least intimidated by her older sister's threat, Nicole did not retreat. She waited for the truth. Losing patience, she stomped her foot.

"Ghost tour tickets and reservations for a midnight séance," Kat admitted.

Slapping her forehead, Nicole whispered to herself, "My sister is a deranged ghost denier!"

Mariah stretched out on her bed, watching Nicole stomp from the luggage to the bathroom and slam the door.

Kat frowned at her friend. "I could've used a little help."

Mariah just chuckled. She often found herself stuck between her warring friends, on opposite sides of the debate about life-after-death. The score was officially one-to-one. Nicole was convinced ghosts walked among the living, but skeptic Kat was determined to prove her sister wrong by seeking out and investigating allegedly haunted locations.

A wise woman, Mariah always refused to be drawn into the paranormal debate, falling back on her stock reply, "I don't have a horse in this race." Taking sides was a lose-lose scenario in the sisters' "ghost wars." Besides, Mariah would have to explain why her vote would be cast for the visitors from beyond the grave. She had kept her ability to communicate with the dead hidden for this long, why complicate her life by revealing the secret now?

Kat busied herself with turning down the covers of the queen bed she would share with her sister and then spent several minutes fluffing and arranging the pillows before climbing in and turning off the light.

At that moment, Mariah wondered how she'd let herself get pulled into "Ghost Hunting with Kat" Season 2. She had to admit that kidnapping Nicole sounded crazy now, but it had made perfect sense at the time. In the dimly lit bar, the two friends had planned each move like mob kingpins. Looking back, it'd probably been the tequila shots.

The conversation between Alice and the Cheshire Cat from her favorite childhood story about Wonderland offered an insight into the rabbit hole where the three now found themselves. She replayed the scene in her head.

*"But I don't want to go among mad people," Alice remarked.*

*"Oh, you can't help that," said the cat. "We're all mad here. I'm mad. You're mad."*

*"How do you know I'm mad?" said Alice.*

*"You must be," said the cat, "or you wouldn't have come here."*

The Cheshire fur ball was right. She must be mad, or why else did she follow the two sisters down the paranormal rabbit hole? Falling, falling, falling… down the deep tunnel, the three had landed in a world frequented by the dead. She had no one to blame but herself for the predicament in which she now found herself. When you go chasing white rabbits, you know you're going to fall.

## Chapter 7

**The** purring of the tabby cat and the persistent sensations of a phantom paw on her shoulder awakened Mariah. She tried ignoring the spirit, but the cat was relentless. Finally, Mariah gave in.

Getting out of bed, she slipped out of the room, leaving her two friends to their dreams. Dressed in flannel pjs, Mariah trailed the ghost cat down the hallway and serpentine staircase from the fourth floor to the deserted lobby. Swinging the east double glass doors open, she stepped onto the veranda where her new friend waited.

And that was how Mariah found herself in the dark on the night of the blue moon. She knew the folklore that swirled around the lunar anomaly. Rare, it only occurred every eighteen to nineteen years on the last days of October. It was truly a spooky time when darkness reigned, and the spirits of the dead wandered aimlessly in the moonlight.

The ghostly feline took off down the cement stairs with a purposeful trot. He was on a mission. At the bottom, he stopped and turned back as if to beckon her before continuing.

The silence of the garden made Mariah pause. There were no sounds. No whisper of wind through the trees overhead, no rustling of fallen leaves scattered on the stone walkway below. Everything felt… still. An unnatural quiet, as if the birds and animals were frozen in fear of predators they could not see.

Gathering her courage, Mariah descended the cement staircase. Reaching the last step, she took a quick glance around the garden. A white mist crept through the vast forest surrounding the hotel. It seeped through the branches and over the treetops, blotting out the stars one by one. Long, twisting fingers of white crawled their way from the forest, laying down a blanket of fog as it inched closer. The moist air clung to her hair and clothing. Mariah wrapped her arms around herself, silently wishing she was back in her room, snuggling under the covers.

Hurrying after the orange tabby, she wondered why this outdoor adventure couldn't wait until the sun was up and the fog had cleared. She finally spied the cat through the white mist, stretched out beside a large stone sticking from a well-maintained grave. A fresh bouquet of flowers marked the burial site, proving the departed one had not been forgotten.

"Well, what do we have here?" she whispered. Curious, Mariah swiped dead leaves from the top of the cold stone. Chalky dust clinging to her fingers, she knelt in the grass quilted with fallen golden maples and curled red oak leaves to read the inscription. The wind, rain, and snow of each passing year had almost erased the words of remembrance.

In loving Memory
Of Morris
May 1973- October 1994

The cat—who was watching from his final resting place. Dark eyes missed nothing.

Finally, Mariah looked up. *How do you comfort a dead cat?* she wondered. Racking her brain for what she knew about animal spirits, she came up with a few facts. Cat spirits were rare; they usually haunted where they had lived and were pretty much harmless.

Her mind flashed on the picture of Morris in the lobby where a memorial to the ginger cat hung. He had earned the title of "General Manager."

Meeting the feline stare, she said, "I get it. You want everyone to know you are still on the job greeting guests, acting as a guide, and keeping the hotel free of mice."

Rising, Mariah saluted the pesky spirit, hoping to motivate the cat to move on to another guest. "Thank you for your service, Morris."

Morris stood. Ears and whiskers pricked forward; he ignored Mariah. Concentrating all his attention on the hotel, he hissed. Low to the ground, hind legs coiled under his body, Morris took off, disappearing into the mist.

Mariah scanned the hotel, searching for what had spooked the ghost cat. Her attention was drawn to the fourth-floor balcony. Someone stepped to the railing—but there was a man whose face she could not see hovering in the shadows.

Mariah jumped, letting out a slight yelp

when the person went over the railing and descended in a cloud of mist. Within the cloud, the figure of a young girl fell slowly to the limestone pavement… then disappeared.

Before it registered what she was doing, Mariah sprinted along the path back to the hotel. All she knew was that she wanted to get out of the mist.

Reaching the stairs to the hotel veranda, she looked back and saw the mysterious fog slowly work its way across the mountaintop, revealing the perfectly safe moonlit court-yard. Her only thought, *This is a place full of dark secrets and hidden skeletons.*

## Chapter 8

**Leaning** against the wrought iron railing, Nicole sipped a pumpkin latte while waiting to be joined by Kat and Mariah. She looked out over the Fountain Garden of the east lawn to the Frisco Sporting Club arena and beyond to the surrounding forest. Autumn in the Ozarks was Nicole's favorite time of year. The leaves were changing colors, the air was crisp, and the weather was perfect for outdoor activities.

Hearing movement from behind, she turned. First through the double doors was a group of women wrapped up in scarves and sweaters, headed for a morning stroll, followed by her sister and friend.

Nicole smiled and pointed to a booth sporting a large yellow, red, and blue circular target and asked, "You two ready to connect with your inner lumberjack?"

Surprised by the turn of events, Kat

accepted the peace offering with a shake of her head.

"So, the little city girl wants to try her hand at hatchet throwing," Mariah mocked, pulling back long shirt sleeves and flexing. "Look at these muscles. The farm has a wood heating stove; I've been chopping wood since I was a kid."

"Impressive, but the secret to hitting the bullseye is all in your form, not your strength," Nicole shot over her shoulder, taking the stairs to the rock walkway below.

Kat and Mariah soon caught up, and Mariah took the lead. Strategically skirting "cat cemetery," she followed the gravel path through the game area where several families competed in a horseshoe-throwing challenge, and a father and daughter enjoyed a chess match on a giant game board.

Kat stopped. "Who's winning?"

The young girl replied, pointing a finger at her chest before making the next move.

"Keep up!" Nicole yelled back at Kat. Steering the group through the outdoor food and drink stands offering burgers, BBQ sandwiches, and shaved ice cones, she located the ax throwing booth.

The attendant met the three guests and

passed along the rules as well as a few tips. Nicole and Mariah politely listened while formulating their own winning strategies.

"I'll go first," Nicole interrupted the young man, taking the hatchet. Gripping the handle with both hands, she brought the ax back over her head. Right foot on the throw line, left just behind, she rocked, weight shifting forward, then back, forward, back. Then, bringing the ax forward again, she let go.

The blade sliced the air and sunk into the board, sticking in the splintered wood just to the right of the third ring.

"I hit it! I hit it!" Nicole let out, clapping as she jumped up and down.

Not impressed, Mariah schooled the novice. "Throwing a tomahawk and hitting the center of the target is all in your arm motion. Watch and learn."

Taking the ax, Mariah stepped to the throwing line and demonstrated her winning technique. "First, it's important to hold the tomahawk correctly. Grip the handle with one hand, giving it a firm, business handshake about an inch or two from the end. Next, stand straight, facing the target. Don't take a step forward or backward as you prepare to throw. Instead, raise the ax over your head, then bring it forward like an overhand football throw," she instructed, releasing the handle.

The tomahawk tumbled end over end, hitting the bull's eye before bouncing to the ground.

"Dull blade!" Mariah shouted in defense, running to the target to inspect the ax.

Nicole doubled over in laughter. Barely able to speak, she mocked her competitor, "So, the little farm girl can't handle the agony of defeat! Tomahawks don't stick into soft-wood targets because they're razor sharp, Mariah. They stick because they're thrown correctly and accurately."

Kat laughed out loud, happy that Nicole was finally having a good time. Pointing to the pellet gun booth, she asked, "Hey, Champ, want to try your luck at target practice?"

Nicole didn't answer right away, but, instead, glanced around the game yard. The sun sparkled through the green, gold, and red canopy of the trees circling the resort. The occasional *caw* of a crow and jeer of a blue jay could be heard off in the woods as a small animal, maybe a squirrel, scrambled through the undergrowth. When a little bit of chilly morning air hit her lungs, she said, "I love autumn." Catching a glimpse of two people with backpacks before they faded into the forest gave her an idea. Grabbing Kat's hand, she maneuvered her toward the trail. "Let's go hiking."

Autumn was a welcome change from the long dog days of an Ozark summer. It added an extra bounce to the three hiker's steps. Feet crunched and swished through piles of dead leaves littering the gravel walking path. The sun on their skin had a very different feeling to that of spring or summer.

With each stride, Nicole's mind became clearer. She stopped to close her eyes and take in a few deep breaths of crisp fall air. With each, she felt more in charge of her life, her mind more alert, her thoughts clearer. She realized it was time to stop looking backward. Her son's death had left her yearning for answers about life and death. She finally realized there *were* no answers. It was time to move forward and leave her obsession with the spirit world behind. She was a woman walking into her own future, a future which lay squarely in her own hands.

Mariah held back for a moment. The pathway threaded through the mountain forest. The swaying shadows of towering trees, side-by-side, lining the path caused her to glance upward in time to catch a glimpse of the morning sun before a dark cloud erased it. The trees swished and creaked in the wind. Leaves scurried along the path and the breeze became sharper, raising goosebumps. *Countless horror movies begin the same way*, she thought, hurrying to catch up.

The *snap* and *crack* of twigs and branches hiding under the carpet of leaves in the forest's shadows became the focus of Mariah's attention. After last night, she worried that, without warning, the monsters of the hotel might be up to something.

After only a few minutes into the hike, the trail came to an abrupt end. Cold clouds appeared when Nicole breathed out. A sudden gust of hundreds of leaves blown in whirlwinds put a halt to the expedition. A twister of leaves danced across the trail and encircled a shed blocking the path. Time seemed to stop.

In those frozen seconds, the wind died, and the tree leaves ceased to rustle.

Dry, dead leaves scurried out of the way as Nicole stepped forward.

Mariah grabbed Nicole's arm to stop her but missed. It was in that moment of absolute stillness when Mariah realized a door was about to open that could not be closed. It was a door that would lead them further down the rabbit hole into the dark history of the Crescent Hotel.

The silence was broken when Nicole read the title carved into the wooden sign tacked to the building, "Baker's Bottle Burial Grave Site."

Curious, she placed a hand on each side of her face and peered through one of the dirty display windows. Hundreds of old bottles, some empty and others half-filled with liquid, littered the deep hole.

Kat joined her sister. "It's a midden.*"*

"What's that? Nicole asked.

"Fancy term archaeologists use for a trash heap," Kat replied while moving around the glass to get a better view.

The funny tingling in Mariah's gut cautioned, *Don't go any closer.* The little voice in her head warned, *What is buried at the bottom of the pit was not meant to be found.*

"Well, I guess it really is true; one man's trash *is* another man's treasure." Nicole chuckled.

Kat backed away from the window, disturbed by the contents of the dark hole. She asked, "Who the hell was Norman Baker?"

## Chapter 9
## Muscatine, Iowa, 1870

**Summoned** to his father's study, Norman found his mother seated in one of the wingback chairs in front of the stone fireplace. Working at his desk, John Baker ignored the presence of his son, and continued reviewing the daily ledger for his machine shop.

Finally, Mr. Baker looked up from the pile of paperwork. He stood with hands behind his back, walked to the front of his desk, then stared at his son.

Norman did not flinch, but his father's controlling gaze left him feeling suffocated and trapped.

Head down, one hand stroking his chin, John Baker paced the room. Finally, he stopped and looked first at his beautiful, dark-haired wife and then at the young boy standing at her side.

The boy knew what was coming; he had

heard the story so many times he knew it by heart. But, before he could speak, his mother gently took his hand in hers and squeezed, warning him to remain silent.

Mr. Baker resumed pacing. "Germany was a mess at the turn of the century. Job shortages, rising taxes, and famine plagued the homeland. Jobless, starving, I had no choice. I left everything to seek a better life in the United States, the land of economic opportunity. I married your mother and moved to Muscatine, where I built the first sheet iron and boiler machine shop in southwestern Iowa."

Mr. Baker stopped in his tracks and looked at his son. "Norman, I have worked hard to provide you with the food you eat and the clothes on your back. All I ask in return is you attend school and study your lessons."

John Baker held up an envelope. He removed and unfolded a single sheet of paper. Waving it in the air, he said, "Professor Roberts, principal of Third Ward School, has notified me of your outstanding attendance record." Baker tossed the letter in the fireplace, where it was quickly consumed by yellow flames.

Mr. Baker took a long breath, struggling to control the irritation bubbling up in his chest. "It seems my son, Norman George Baker, has earned the distinction of having played hooky more times than any other pupil in the history of the school."

Norman could think of nothing to say in his defense. School was boring. It was more fun sneaking into his father's machine shop and playing impish pranks on the workmen, which, to his delight, usually ended in him being chased along the railroad tracks by angry workers.

Furious, Norman stomped his foot. "Papa, I don't want to go to school; I want to be a machinist like you. There's nothing I can learn in school that will help me in a machine shop."

"You *will* complete school and go to college as your brothers and sisters have not." Hoping to convince his son, Mr. Baker said, "Norman, you can have your pick of any college in the world."

Norman was resentful of his father's controlling nature. "Papa, I don't want to go to college."

"Ach! When I tell you to go to college, you go. There is no answering back in this family."

The youngest of ten children, pet of the

family, Norman ran to his mother and pleaded, "Mama, please don't send me away to college."

Mr. Baker grabbed his son by the arm and raised his hand to strike the boy.

Norman was shocked. What was happening? Adored and pampered by his parents, spoiled by his older brothers and sisters, he'd been made to feel special all his life. His papa had never raised a hand to him. Why couldn't his parents understand he didn't like school and didn't want to sit in a boring classroom, learning about things he had no interest in studying?

Norman broke free. He ran from the room and out of the house with his father hot on his heels. Coming to the wire fence between the yard and the pasture, Norman dropped to the ground and rolled beneath.

Not to be out done by his son, Mr. Baker crept beneath the fence and made an attempt to grab the boy.

Norman, determined to not get a whipping, quickly rolled back to the other side. The two kept this up until, disgusted and beaten, Mr. Baker abandoned the effort, stomped to the house, then slammed the screen door shut.

In the end, Norman managed to get his wish. To the great disappointment of John Baker, his son did not attend college. Instead, Norman dropped out of school after the tenth grade, set on following in his father's footsteps and becoming a machinist.

It wasn't long before he was accepted by Kerr's Machine shop in Muscatine as an apprentice. His job consisted of sweeping the floor, firing up the boiler, and running the engines, but he didn't mind. Eventually, he was allowed to operate the machines used in the factory to make metal parts for other machines. Then, a random event changed the course of the young machinist's life forever.

## Chapter 10
## Muscatine, Iowa, 1904

**At** the turn of the century, the Wright Brothers made their first successful flight, Henry Ford created the first automobile that middle-class Americans could afford, and thousands of people packed theaters each night to see the amazing acts of vaudeville.

Out of sight of the audience, Norman Baker stood off-stage in the wings. So intrigued by travelling shows presenting "mentalists" and other vaudeville performers to the public, he'd set up his own troupe of singers, plate spinners, ventriloquists, and acrobats. As Charles Welch, he traveled the country with his wife as mind-reader, Pearl Tangley.

Looking out at the crowded theater, Norman marveled at how one random event had steered his life in an unexpected direction. As fate would have it, his life had taken a sudden detour after Herbert L. Flint, the stage hypnotist, had brought his vaudeville performance to Muscatine, Iowa.

At the time, Norman had taken a part-time job as a circus barker, promoting a two-headed calf and other oddities. To his surprise, he'd liked performing and had quickly learned the tricks of the trade. First, he would draw in passing pedestrians to the booth with, "Hurry… Hurry… Hurry, folks! Get your tickets here." Once he had attracted a crowd, Norman would launch into a well-practiced spiel. "Ladies and gentlemen, you're about to behold a sight so strange, so disturbing, so utterly monstrous, that I urge you who are easily frightened or upset, who suffer from nervous disorders or weak hearts, to forgo entering this exhibit."

One night, on his way home from the circus, Norman had noticed a poster advertising Flint's stage show. He'd decided to attend. He'd found the performance of the power of mental suggestion intriguing. Recovering from a resent serious illness, he'd been certain his mental abilities had helped heal him and he'd wanted to learn more.

Flint brought his twenty-year-old daughter, Marina, on stage. "You feel very sleepy…"

he'd said. With these words, the stage hypnotist had cast his spell over the petite young woman.

Marina had been placed on the floor and instructed to act as stiff as a board. Two audience volunteers had lifted the now-rigid girl and placed her across the backs of two wooden chairs, feet resting on one, head and neck on another. A third chair was placed under the young woman's posterior.

Marina had then been told that her body would become as firm as a plank, allowing her to be suspended between the chairs. Then, to everyone's amazement, Flint had pulled away the middle chair, leaving the young woman stiff and suspended between the remaining chairs.

Flint had then invited an audience member onstage to break a large cement block placed on the catatonic girl's body with a sledgehammer. The stone split and fell to the stage with one powerful hit. Marina had then been placed back onto the floor. Upon Flint's instructions, his daughter had woken, stood, and smiled out at the cheering crowd.

Curiously inquisitive about the strange power of mind-over-matter demonstrated by the stage hypnotist, Norman had begun exploring healing through thought control and the power of suggestion. He'd enrolled in a correspondence course on mind control. He'd begun to acquire a library on the subject, and when he'd fallen seriously ill and hadn't been expected to live more than a few days, it hadn't been the doctors with their pills and potions that had saved him. Norman was certain it'd been the power of his own mind.

Norman Baker had been so inspired that he'd aggressively pursued his goal of producing a bigger and better version of Flint's magic act. After a disappointing slow start, his show had taken off and become a hit on the vaudeville circuit. Baker's mentalist show ran successfully for a decade before his career had taken another unforeseen turn.

## Chapter 11
## Muscatine, Iowa, 1929

**Norman** Baker loosened his lavender tie and rolled up the sleeves of his white shirt. Ready to get down to work, he swiveled from one side to the other of the hexagon-shaped desk, scanning reports and shuffling paperwork. Each section was delegated to a different successful business enterprise, making it easy to manage his vast empire.

Hands behind head, he leaned back in the chair, reflecting on all he had accomplished in such a short time. At this moment in his life, it could be argued that he was an innovative businessman with theatrical experience, machinery skills, as well as the ability and drive to capitalize on these attributes.

Thinking back on his life, he realized it had all begun with the return to Muscatine after ten successful years traveling the country, performing his mentalist act. Taking a summer break before the fall opening in Chicago, he'd returned to Muscatine accompanied by his wife, Theresa. The decision made him a very wealthy man.

Realizing the importance of self-promotion in show business, Norman had desired a musical instrument be used for outdoor advertising of his vaudeville magical act. Encouraged by his wife, who was a pianist, he'd begun tinkering around in his brother's machine shop, of which he was part owner. Though he had no musical education, it hadn't been long before he'd come up with a portable organ that ran on air pressure, a variation of the popular steam organ. He'd named his invention the Tangley Air Calliope.

Norman marveled at how quickly his invention had caught the attention of the entertainment industry. He'd sold the first calliope for five hundred dollars, and quickly took orders for more. The portable organ had soon been in much demand from carnivals and circuses. A year later, he'd been making more than $200,000. By the next year, Norman had closed his vaudeville show, opened a factory in Muscatine devoted to building air organs, and divorced his wife.

Riding on a wave of much-deserved success, he'd been devastated at the next turn of events. Fire completely destroyed the calliope factory. Touring the destruction, he'd happened upon a traveling artist who was tinting photographs. Fascinated with the process, he'd paid the artist to teach him the technique. Recognizing the money-making potential, he started the Tangley School of Art, teaching others the process. The art school venture earned him a hefty $75,000.00 in just over three years, which was put to good use in rebuilding the air-organ factory.

Norman pushed aside a stack of his weekly newspaper, the *Midwest Free Press*, where he had accused the overlords of the aluminum industry of poisoning Americans. In the article, he'd attributed the rise of cancer death rates to the use of aluminum in baking powder, city water purification, and cooking utensils.

Under the pile of newspapers, he noticed the latest edition of his *TNT Magazine*. Picking it up, he flipped through the thirty-six pages of advertisements featuring everything a person could want, ranging from alarm clocks, lamps, and car batteries to cans of beans and cigars.

Tossing it to the side, he turned off the radio, then, walking to the window, he peered out into the night. Radio provided cheap entertainment. Besides live music, sports programs, and weather forecasts, radio also broadcast advertisements.

Realizing the business opportunity, Norman had wanted in on the action. So, he'd nego-tiated a deal with the Muscatine Chamber of Commerce. He'd promised to broadcast "real, honest-to-goodness" entertainment that farm-ers and small-town folks would enjoy in ex-change for free rent and utilities for the station.

Getting the go-ahead on his new venture, Norman had set out to choose the call name of the station. Wise to the ins and outs of broadcasting, he'd realized the four-letter combination had to be unique, something that would make his station stand out. Radio stations east of the Mississippi River had to start their stations with 'W,' and stations west of the Mississippi with 'K,' so that left him with three letters to choose from the twenty-six-letter alphabet. Working with a variety of letter combinations, he'd finally settled on TNT. The letters would be perfect for the explosive broadcasts he'd planned to air from Iowa.

K-TNT had gone on the air on Thanksgiving Day, 1925 with the call letters touted as the abbreviation for "**K**now **T**he **N**aked **T**ruth." Norman built the station on the highest hill of the city and eventually had added a gift shop, a restaurant, an excursion boat ride on the nearby lake, and a large, six-pump gas station.

With a lineup of live music, agricultural reports, and his colorful broadcasts, K-TNT had become popular among rural Mid-westerners. Many of his audience had flocked to Muscatine on summer Sundays to picnic outside the radio studio where they could enjoy listening to the live broadcasts. He'd gained further influence by broadcasting on behalf of Herbert Hoover's presidential cam-paign. The president had later repaid Baker by pushing a button from the White House, ceremoniously staring the newspaper presses, launching the *Midwest Free Press.*

It'd seemed as if he could do no wrong. The popularity of Tangley Air Calliope sky-rocketing, radio career booming, magazine and newspaper thriving, his many successful business ventures had propelled the high school dropout to millionaire status.

A line from a William Shakespeare play came to mind as he stood and went to the window and looked out into the night. "Be not afraid of greatness; some are born great, some achieve greatness, and others have greatness thrust upon them."

## Chapter 12

**The** SkyBar was packed. The cozy rooftop restaurant stretched the length of the fourth floor. Laughter from within could be heard outside where Nicole, Kat, and Mariah stood. The tinkle of glass, the cool *clink* of ice, and the fizz of soda greeted them at the entrance.

Kat requested a table for five on the veranda. The hostess threaded a path for the three guests around the corner bar lined with wine, beer, and signature cocktails placed on square napkins. Patrons stood or sat on wooden stools, sampling the wares, laughing with friends, or watching sports on the big screen TV. The bartender, busy interacting with customers, taking orders, and serving drinks, managed a quick welcoming wink as they passed.

Kat glimpsed the young chess player from the Frisco Sporting Club eating pizza with her father. The girl smiled and waved as Kat passed.

The hostess, on a mission to get the new patrons seated quickly, urged the three women forward. Opening the double doors, she escorted her charges to the balcony where diners relaxed while being entertained by the birds feeding off pizza crumbs.

Once seated, Nicole took in the breathtaking view, the sky above and the Ozark Mountains below. The oak and maple trees were shades of red, while the elm, poplar, hickory, and redbud had turned hues of gold and yellow. She had to admit that Eureka Springs was the perfect place for a fall getaway.

Catching Kat's eye, she asked, "Table for five?"

Mariah was wondering the same thing, "Why the secrecy? It's not like you're some government agent trying to protect sources and methods."

Nicole added, "Besides, secrets require discretion and judgment, which my abduct-tion to 'scary town' proves you lack."

"All right… It's not a secret. Think of it more as a surprise," she pleaded. Digging her phone from a back pocket, Kat scrolled.

"While you two were enjoying the hot tub at the New Moon Spa, I have been doing some research on the mystery man, Norman Baker.

"Of course, you have," Nicole said, not happy with her sister. "You just can't help yourself. It's the scientist in you: research and investigate, always searching for answers. When will you learn that science doesn't have all the answers?"

Not in the least put off by Nicole's rant since it was not unusual for her sister to go off the rails at least once a day, Kat kept scrolling. Finally finding what she was searching for, Kat turned the screen from Nicole to Mariah and demanded, "Look."

Leaning forward, the two stared at the screen, then up at Kat. In unison, they asked, "A bible?"

More than a little irritated, Nicole confronted Kat, "Well, my understanding of Christianity is that it takes more than a picture of a bible on your phone to absolve a person of their indiscretions... which you seem to relish collecting."

"Hey, can we please discuss my perceived lapses in judgement later?" Kat asked, trying to get Nicole off her back and focused on the picture. "This isn't just any bible. Look closer," Kat insisted, pointing to the printing on the front of the worn book.

Nicole and Mariah took another look while Kat explained. "The Gideons are a Christian group. For over a hundred years, they have placed bibles in hotels all over the United States."

"And?" Nicole asked, demanding more details.

Kat scrolled to the next picture. "This is the first page of the book."

Nicole took the phone for a closer look. The page, brown with age, was blank except for the printing at the bottom. As she read, Nicole ran a finger along the two lines of black print.

NORMAN BAKER INC
Eureka Springs, Ark

"So, how does that explain the magic number five seating arrangement?" Nicole asked, pointing to the two extra chairs at the table.

"I contacted the owner of this book," Kat announced, "and learned that the Gideons received permission to place bibles at the Crescent Hotel sometime during the late

1930s by… Norman Baker. The owner of the book claims it came from one of the rooms. Smiling her satisfaction at the surprised looks of her two critics, Kat pleaded her case, "Don't you see, this may be the clue we need to unravel the twisted connection between this mystery man named Norman Baker, the bottle dump, and the Crescent Hotel."

Standing, she waved at a woman and young man approaching the table. "Oh, and the two extra seats are for our lunch guests."

## Chapter 13
## Muscatine, Iowa, 1929

**Norman** Baker signed off the nightly K-TNT broadcast with background music from his calliope. The evening show aired during dinner hour, when most people would be at home, listening to the radio. The evening program featured an excellent lineup of live music, agricultural reports, and his own colorful reporting and commentary on stories of local interest to his listeners.

Capitalizing on the growing distrust felt toward big government and big business, he enjoyed the role of hero-savior for Muscatine's common folk. Using the radio as a platform to crusade for small businesses, farmers, and laborers, his popularity and business profits soared.

Rolling up the sleeves of the white shirt, he recounted the business decisions that brought him to this moment. Always on the alert for matters of public interest, he'd decided to investigate when it'd been brought to his attention that a local doctor, Dr. Baerwald, had been in a fight with the medical community. The doctor had claimed to have a cure for varicose veins, a painless injection of herbs. The medical establishment had labeled the doctor a fake, claiming a cure for varicose veins did not exist. They'd stood by their claim that the only treatment was removing part of the damaged vein or using elastic bandages to keep the vein from protruding too much.

After meeting with Dr. Baerwald and interviewing some of his patients, Norman had been convinced the cure worked. Realizing a business opportunity when one was presented, he'd gone into partnership with the doctor and had started the Tangley Institute, a hospital in Muscatine.

He had to smile at the unintended consequences of the attacks that'd followed from the American Medical Association. Labeled a quack with a fake cure, his response had been quick and effective. Railing against the unwarranted attacks during the nightly broadcasts, he'd claimed doctors were motivated by greed. He'd refused to share Dr. Baerwald's secret formula with the medical community.

Despite the criticism and unwarranted con-
demnation from the AMA, the hospital had
been a success, and it hadn't been long before
he'd started to look for another cause to
champion.

A year later, he'd learned of an alleged
cancer cure invented by Dr. Charles Ozias.
The doctor had operated a hospital in
Kansas City. He'd claimed his formula, a
secret blend of herbs and spices, could be
administered by injection and cure one of the
most dreaded of all diseases, cancer. After
testing the cure on five volunteers, Norman
had obtained the "formula" from Dr. Ozias
and started using it as a treatment for cancer
at the Tangley Institute.

Knowing even an incurable disease such
as cancer had a morbid fascination for many,
he'd immediately begun an advertising cam-
paign. *TNT Magazine* published an article on
the front page under the headline, "Cancer is
Cured." Next, K-TNT Radio had announced
that the Tangley Institute, staffed with eleven
physicians and fifty nurses, now had cures
for five ailments declared incurable by the
medical community, including varicose veins
and cancer. Formula #5 cure had been
marketed as "Baker's Magic Elixir," an all-

natural cancer treatment. After each patient had been pronounced cured, he'd encouraged them to share their story over K-TNT.

Hearing those emotional testimonies, hundreds of cancer sufferers flocked to Muscatine seeking relief. The hundred-bed hospital had filled quickly, and many patients had been forced to live in hotels and rooming houses, coming to the hospital daily for treatment.

Denounced as unethical and villainized as a quack with no medical training by the American Medical Association, Norman had taken to the airways, again, to defend his reputation. He'd styled himself as a "self-taught healer" who had spent years investigating health issues, folk remedies, and the power of the mind in healing. He'd used his platform to warn against the hunger of doctors who wanted to squeeze every last dime from common folk for treatments that did not help. He'd claimed the AMA had wanted to buy his cure to take it off the market and force cancer patients into expensive treatments that did not work, such as surgery, radium, and X-ray.

Norman let out a slow chuckle; the efforts to silence him backfired. Despite the very public battle with the medical community, desperate cancer sufferers had continued to flock to Muscatine, and the hospital had become financially successful, earning over four hundred thousand dollars in the first year.

## Chapter 14
## Muscatine, Iowa, 1930

**Hunched** over his desk, a small lamp illuminating the ledger, Norman Baker reviewed the Monday night receipts. A smile tugged at the corner of his mouth; the crowd of fifty thousand had brought in record sales.

The cancer treatment and the hospital had attracted attention across the continent. In an attempt to boost his credibility and alleviate any doubts about the validity of his "Magic Elixir," Norman had decided to build a lawn studio from which to broadcast and perform open-air demonstrations of the treatment. The idea proved to be a wise business decision.

Puffing on a cigar, he rose from his chair. Straightening the lavender tie, and adjusting purple suspenders, he walked to the wall of glass panes and looked out over the hillside. Just a few hours earlier, thousands had gathered on the lawn of the radio station. Under the shade of a huge circus tent, visitors had enjoyed live entertainment, eagerly waiting for the main event. While enjoying the county fair atmosphere, many had broken out their pocketbooks and splurged on souvenirs from the gift store and hotdogs from one of the outdoor vendors or purchased cheap fuel from the K-TNT gas station.

Baker smiled, remembering the boister-ous applause that'd broken out when he'd taken the stage clad in his trademark white suit and lavender tie. A born performer and a savvy businessman, he knew the import-ance of branding. The audience would have been disappointed if he had appeared in a regular suit and tie. Removing the white hat from his head, he'd waved it at the crowd then walked to the microphone.

After welcoming the visitors to the K-TNT out-door studio, he'd launched into a well-thought-out attack on his enemies, taking a swipe at the American Medical Association. "The medical octopus of organized medicine is the greatest roadblock in finding a cure for cancer. One hundred and forty thousand people die every year in the United States from the dreaded disease. Our illustrious medical community admits that it does not know what causes cancer, how it spreads, or how to cure sufferers. Yet, they continue to recommend three treatments that never cure but *cause* the patient more pain: operations that mutilate and X-ray and radium that burn."

He paused to make eye contact with several in the audience, then said, "I know it's a relief for Americans across this great nation to learn that, if you ever have cancer, my treatment and hospital can heal the dreaded disease."

When the applause had died down, he'd invited former cancer patients of the institute to join him on the stage to tell their stories. He'd encouraged each volunteer to tell how they'd come to the institute, how the treatment had been administered, and how the "Magic Elixir" had cured them.

After the last volunteer had left the stage, Norman Baker set out to prove to the live audience that his "Magic Elixir," secret Formula#5, was a safe treatment that killed only cancerous tumors.

Taking a bottle of black-colored liquid from his pocket, he'd held it up for the crowd and said, "This is the very same elixir used at the institute to cure cancer." To the amazement of his audience, Norman had then unscrewed the cap and swallowed the entire contents.

For a few brief moments, the stunned crowd had merely stared and waited.

When Norman had appeared unaffected by the ingestion of the liquid, a round of deafening applause erupted around the stage.

Basking in the approval of his fans, Baker had prepared for the program's grand finale by uncovering a tray of medical instruments. Looking out at the crowd that had covered the hillside and the thousands of cars surrounding the radio station, he'd welcomed Mandus Johnson on stage. "Mr. Johnson has a brain tumor. I will cure the cancer without pain, without the loss of blood, and without damaging the surrounding healthy tissue."

The crowd had surged forward. Gasps of horror had risen from the audience as Norman proceeded to surgically remove the top half of Johnson's skull. Appalled, several near the stage had fainted. Seemingly unfazed by the reaction of the crowd, Baker had applied the formula and replaced the previously removed section of the patient's skull. Fully conscious, Mandus had smiled and waved. Turning to the audience, Baker had thrown both hands into the air and announced, "Mr. Johnson is cured."

Across the lawn and all the way up the hillside, word of the miracle had spread like wildfire. The crowd had clapped, stomped, and chanted, "Dr. Baker, Dr. Baker, Dr. Baker," as the self-taught healer had bowed, then left the stage.

## Chapter 15
## Muscatine, Iowa, 1931

**Norman** Baker slumped in the chair, exhausted. Elbows resting on his desk, head in hands, he let out a frustrated sigh. He shook his head and sat up. Smoothing back silver hair, he stared at the revolver on his desk. His mind flashed on the disastrous events of the past few months.

Thinking back, he guessed it'd all begun with the Federal Radio Commission being in cahoots with the medical octopus, trying to shut down his cancer and health talks by allocating K-TNT's evening on-air hours to a station in Philadelphia. Determined to get his time back, he'd lodged a formal complaint, insisting the commission was trying to close down all independent stations. He'd presented his case at a hearing in Washington D.C., with no results. He'd then traveled to De Moines where he'd attended a conference called by the Federal Radio Commission to discuss radio broadcasting concerns, where he'd, once again, confronted the commissioners. This time, his presentation had been a success. He'd returned home with permission to broadcast from sunrise to sunset and from 11 PM to 1 AM.

Baker had installed a microphone in his office at the hospital and had begun his late-night broadcast from that location. Not long after, he'd started getting unsigned, threatening letters. Since his nightly habits were well-known in the town, friends and associates had urged him to not be on the streets or in his automobile late at night.

Refusing to be intimidated, he'd started carrying a revolver, and had boldly continued to walk down to the K-TNT Café after the 1 PM broadcast. Over a cup of coffee, he would read the area's daily papers. Around 2 AM, he would stroll down to the riverbank to check on his boat, then return to either his apartment at the K-TNT radio station or to his private room at the hospital. When his staff had reported seeing several unsavory characters prowling around the hospital and the radio station, his watchmen and hospital executives had received permission to also arm themselves.

A few months later, in April, the unthinkable had happened. At midnight, as usual, he'd begun the late-night show from the microphone in his hospital office. Just minutes after signing off, the phone on his desk had rung. It'd been the night watchman.

"Boss, better not come down to the café tonight. There are three tough-looking guys parked across the street."

Baker had relayed the message to several of the hospital staff who had joined him for a late-night meeting. They'd all laughed and joked about the absurdity of a gang of thugs in Muscatine as they'd prepared to head down to the café.

When a dog near the hospital had started a violent fit of barking, Baker had sensed something was wrong. Peering out the open window, he'd seen flashes of light as gunfire erupted, *pop-pop-pop*. The whistling of bullets and splintering of glass had caused chaos in the office. "Get down!" he'd yelled, then switched off the lights, leaving the room in total darkness.

Baker had scrambled through the rubble and grabbed the gun from the desk. The reverberating sound of the gunfire had filled the room as he'd emptied the .38 automatic, hitting one of the gunmen. In the silence that'd followed, the staff had gathered behind Baker. From the shattered window, they'd watched two of the prowlers help the third to an auto waiting in the alley behind the hospital.

The attack hadn't been over. Shortly before three o'clock, Baker had gotten a call from the night watchman at the radio station. "Mr. Baker, somebody just threw two bombs at the station. I shot at the bombers before they disappeared down the hill, but, sorry, sir, I failed to hit any of them."

Hanging up, Baker had brought one clenched fist down onto his desk, scattering papers across the room. If the medical elite thought they could intimidate him by shooting up his hospital and dynamiting his radio station, they were in for a big surprise.

The next day, he'd secured permission to place a machine gun at both locations. The hospital and station had now become armed fortresses.

In the days that'd followed, his enemies had tried their best to cause a scandal by doubling their efforts to discredit his cancer cure and ruin his reputation. The American Medical Association, the Iowa State Medical Society, the Muscatine County Medical Association, and the Iowa Health Board had aligned against him. A barrage of articles in the Iowa newspapers and magazines had appeared, stating that he'd been a cancer fake and a quack who should be jailed for tricking cancer patients into believing they could be cured and then charging them for the bogus cure.

One month later, he'd held a second open-air broadcast in an effort to defend his reputation. Before noon, thousands of people had already gathered on the radio station's lawn. After Governor Hammill's speech, over thirty patients who were being cured or had been cured appeared, one-by-one on stage.

With each testimony, the crowd had surged closer and closer. Last, had come Mandus Johnson himself. Since that first demonstration in which the top of his skull had been removed and the cancer treated, a membrane had grown over the affected area, protecting his brain.

The enthusiastic response of the crowd had gone on for several minutes. At the end, a former patient had stepped forward and patted Baker on the back. Turning to the tens of thousands of onlookers, he'd proclaimed,

"Behold, the man who saved mankind from the hideous scourge of cancer."

One day after the demonstration, Baker had been charged with practicing medicine and performing surgery without a license. The battle in court had lasted nine days. When questioned, he'd explained, "It's true, I am not a doctor. I did not treat patients at the Tangley Institute. I hired licensed physicians and surgeons to care for the patients. As I said before, I merely owned the hospital." At the end of the trial, Baker had been found not guilty.

Members of organized medicine had refused to give up. Convincing the Federal Radio Commission to revoke K-TNT Radio Station license, they'd taken their case against Baker to the Iowa Supreme Court.

Confident that he would win again, Norman hadn't been prepared for the verdict. Overwhelmed, he'd listened in stunned silence as the jury foreman had read the verdict.

"We, the jury, find Norman Baker guilty of practicing medicine in the state of Iowa without a license."

When asked by the judge if he'd had anything to say, Baker had thought for a moment of the gross miscarriage of justice that had just taken place in the highest court in the state. *After all I have done, the sacrifice, long hours, and hard work, my seven hundred-and fifty-thousand-dollar business is now shot to hell.* Straightening his shoulders, holding back his true feelings, he'd looked the judge directly in the eye and answered, "No, Your Honor."

With a stern gaze and firm voice, the judge had announced, "It is the judgment and order of the Court that the defendant, Norman Baker, be imprisoned in jail for the term and period of four months, and he pay to the United States of America a fine of two thousand dollars."

## Chapter 16

**Kat** greeted her mystery guests like long-lost friends. Turning to the two seated at the table, she made the introduction, "Nicole and Mariah, this is Ann Rhoden and her son."

Mariah looked at Nicole with raised eyebrows, then back at Kat, waiting for the drama to unfold. It was obvious to Mariah that the theater classes Kat had taken in college were finally paying off.

Ann placed a brown paper bag on the table before taking her seat. "It seems the five of us have a common interest," she explained.

Eyes on the bag, Mariah took the bait. "And what might that be?"

Ann replied, "Norman Baker."

Looking directly at her sister, Kat explained, "I was doing some internet research on Baker and just happened to run across a Facebook post by Ann that I thought might aid us in our investigation of the hotel."

Nicole let out a long breath before speaking. "I believe this is your gig. I'm just a hostage."

Mariah piped in, "And I'm just your getaway driver."

Confused, mother and son looked from Kat, to Nicole, to Mariah, and then back at Kat.

"Don't pay any attention to them," Kat said, smiling at Nicole. "They never want to have any fun."

Looking around the table, Ann began, "It all happened in 1967. During the winter months, the hotel had been closed. There was a caretaker and a few workers who'd stayed on to refurbish the rooms. They'd all been in the kitchen having coffee together and getting ready to go to work. It was early morning, and they must have had the fireplace going.

"Down the hill from the hotel, the priest at St. Elizabeth Catholic Church was reported to have been the first to see the black clouds. About the same time, the mail carrier had arrived, and, seeing the smoke, dashed into the building to warn the workers. He'd been surprised to find the crew still in the kitchen, drinking coffee, unaware of the fire raging on the fourth floor.

"The fire got the tower, the north penthouse, and all the rooms in the center of the fourth floor on the east side, including the SkyBar, then referred to as Dr. Baker's Lounge."

Ann rummaged in the brown bag, withdrew a worn, brown-leather book, then placed it onto the table.

"What's this?" Nicole asked.

"More clues," Kat answered in her best detective voice.

Ann explained, "My mother passed recently. I found this book while going through her belongings. She helped with the cleanup after the fire on the fourth floor."

Nicole picked up the book and read the gold inlaid words on the cover aloud.

"Placed in this Room
By The Gideons
The Property of the Gideons"

More confused than ever, Nicole looked to her sister's guest for an explanation.

"This book was not left behind by a guest or placed in a room haphazardly. Nearly a hundred years ago, a religious organization called the Gideons began distributing bibles in hotel rooms in hopes of spreading the faith to weary travelers."

Mariah took the bible from Nicole. Flipping through the pages, she was surprised when a yellowed, ragged piece of paper fluttered from the book. Time seemed to slow as it drifted on to the tabletop. Everyone scooted closer for a better view.

Nicole struggled to read the scribbled writing. "'I entered the hospital for treatment on… March 23, 1939, and stayed until… April 12. Sure was helped by both treatments. Stayed 7 weeks. Walker Robinson Jackson, Kentucky.'"

The note ended oddly with one last sentence scrawled across the bottom, "O, Lord, give me strength!"

Closing her eyes, Nicole placed fingertips on her temples and gently massaged. Instead of solving the mystery of "Who was Norman Baker?" the story of the Gideon Bible and the fourth-floor fire only raised more questions.

## Chapter 17
## Eureka Springs, Arkansas-1937

**The** purple Franklin Roadster navigated the winding street to the top of Crescent Mountain and rolled to a stop in front of an impressive stone structure. Two guards, each armed with a machine gun and leading a large Doberman, waited to assist the driver.

One guard moved forward and greeted the man as he stepped from the custom-built air-conditioned automobile. "Welcome back to Arkansas, Doctor. How was your trip to Mexico?"

A smile lit Norman Baker's face. A year earlier, he'd been able to work out a deal with the state of Iowa, where he would only serve one day of his four-month jail sentence. After his triumphant release, Lady Luck had chosen to shine on him once again.

"Better than expected," he responded. Being run out of Iowa had not been the crushing blow his enemies had hoped. In fact, it had backfired. He'd obtained permission from the president of Mexico to operate a radio station in Nuevo Laredo on the Rio Grande. Called a "border blaster," the station broadcasted nightly. Operating outside the U.S. Federal Communications Commission's reach, X-ENT was now considered the most powerful station in North America.

Baker stepped onto the red carpet and stared at the imposing structure of stone. He still could not believe his good fortune. After serving the jail sentence, but no longer able to run the Muscatine Institute, he'd set his sights on someplace where he could be back in business, free from the burdensome government regulations he'd faced in Iowa.

After years of searching and miles of travel, he'd heard about a massive forgotten stone castle, previously a haven for the rich which had fallen into disrepair due to the economic hard times of the past few years. He'd hastened to investigate and when he'd gazed up at that beautiful stone structure atop the Ozark Mountains, he'd realized he had found the perfect place for the new home of the Baker Hospital.

After purchasing the property, he'd moved all his staff, along with a hundred and forty patients, from the Muscatine Hospital to Eureka Springs. When the doors of the cancer clinic had opened, hundreds had rushed to the mountaintop to meet Dr. Baker and see what was hailed as the "Castle in the Air" and to receive one of his miracle treatments.

Taking a minute to straighten his white suit jacket and to adjust the purple tie sporting a diamond horseshoe, he breathed in the fresh mountain air laden with the scent of pine. He took a moment to look up at his magnificent castle in the air. The lookout tower on the roof provided a view across the Ozark Mountains into four states. The valley below, with its famous springs, provided a constant supply of healthy mineral water.

Spirits high, Norman climbed the steps to the glass-paned double doors. He removed the white hat and smoothed back silver hair before entering Baker Cancer Clinic.

On the way to the elevator, he gazed briefly into the lobby. Patients, young and old, sat chatting or resting contently, enjoying the cheerful interior painted lavender—his favorite color—and detailed in the carnival-like colors of red, yellow, orange, and black. The look on their faces confirmed the fifty grand in renovations had been a good investment.

Arriving at his penthouse on the fourth floor, he found members of the hospital's senior staff assembled for the weekly meeting. Removing the white suit jacket, he hung it over the back of the desk chair. Hands clasped behind his back, Baker paced as each report was read and discussed.

The last report was presented by Thelma Yount, his new financial advisor. His hypnotic blue eyes stared intently at the new member of the hospital team, waiting impatiently for her report on the health of the overall "business."

Wanting desperately to please her very handsome employer, Miss Yount picked up a flyer that was being mailed across the United States and passed it to her boss. "Sir, the hospital has raked in extraordinary revenues since the latest advertising campaign."

Baker took the mailer and looked it over. The colorful brochure referred to Eureka Springs as the "Switzerland of America" and the Baker Cancer Clinic as a place "Where Sick Folks Get Well."

Thelma was rewarded with a warm and charming smile when she pronounced, "The Baker Cancer Clinic is on track to clear about half a million dollars this year."

## Chapter 18

**The** double doors closed behind Nicole, Kat, and Mariah, muffling the sounds from the SkyBar. "Well, I have to admit, the meeting with Ann Rhoden was very interesting," Mariah began, then stopped, noticing Nicole's frantic search of her pants pockets.

"Hey, I left my phone in the room, I don't want to head downtown without it," Nicole said. Motioning for the two, she led the way down the fourth-floor hall, away from the crowd at the restaurant entrance.

Kat started to follow but was jostled backward several steps by the long line of hungry guests maneuvering to get their names on the waitlist. Standing on tiptoes, looking over a sea of bobbing heads, her eyes were drawn to a glare reflecting off the glass of the photographs hanging on the opposite wall.

*Strange,* she thought, looking overhead

then back to the display. *Must be the ceiling lights reflecting off the glass.*

"Excuse me," she interrupted the hostess taking reservations. "What's all that about?" she asked, pointing to the display of framed pictures and newspaper articles that ran the entire length of the hotel hallway.

The hostess looked up from the black book resting on the reservation podium. "Oh, that's the hotel archives. It tells the history of the resort from its inception to the present."

Thanking the hostess, Kat made her way around the waiting guests to the archives. Quickly scanning the display, her eyes landed on a newspaper ad. "Where Sick Folks Get Well" was plastered across the top. She had discovered a treasure trove of information that might shed some light on the Norman Baker mystery.

The search for facts was interrupted by the annoying repetition of her name, "Kat! Kat!"

Looking up to see Mariah waving impatiently, Kat put the investigative reading on hold and hurried to join her friend.

Ahead of Kat and Mariah, Nicole took a right and almost ran into a woman fumbling for her keys outside room 419. Thinking the woman was lost, she asked, "Can I help you?"

The woman looked up; her cold gaze fixed on Nicole. Turning the key, the door opened, and she disappeared inside. Before Nicole could stop the intruder, the door slammed shut.

Kat and Mariah found Nicole looking from the key in her hand to the room number posted above the door.

"What are you waiting for? Open the door." Kat demanded.

Eyes full of shock, Nicole turned and said, "I just saw a woman enter our room."

"What?" Kat questioned, grabbing the key and opening the door. "Hey, anyone in here?" she asked. Searching and finding no intruder, Kat yelled from the bedroom, "No scary monsters here! Now, get your phone, and let's go."

Kat returned to the sitting room to find Nicole and Mariah standing where she had left them. "Why are you just standing there?"

In disbelief, Nicole confronted her sister. "A strange woman walks into our room and just vanishes; you don't find that cause to pause and assess the situation?"

Kat was saved from answering by Mariah.

"Look around. The beds are made, wet towels have disappeared, and our bags are packed and stacked in the center of the room."

Baffled, Kat took a closer look at the room and then asked Mariah, "What happened to the 'Do Not Disturb' sign we hung outside our door for housekeeping?"

Mariah checked the door and held up the sign, "Still here."

Kat walked to the coffee table in the sitting room. The coins she had carelessly tossed to the table before leaving for their lunch date were now neatly arranged in a straight row, beginning with a stack of quarters, then dimes, nickels, and pennies.

"Why did housekeeping clean our room when we specifically requested, they don't?" she wondered aloud.

Mariah held up the towel and tissue basket she had found in the hall near the door. "Nope, don't think it was housekeeping."

"Well, who then?" Kat asked.

Something about the woman bothered Nicole. Then she realized what it was. Rushing to the picture on the wall, she pulled the towel away. The woman in the hall was the woman in the photograph. "It was Theodora," Nicole announced.

"It couldn't have been Theodora," Kat insisted.

"And why not?" Nicole demanded.

"Because… Theodora is DEAD!" Kat shouted, out of patience.

"Exactly. That is why you didn't find anyone hiding in our room. Theodora is a ghost!" Nicole shouted, losing patience with her sister.

Determined to clear up the housekeeping mystery and ghost theory, Kat marched to the phone and rang the front desk.

"The Crescent Hotel, the most fun place in Eureka Springs," the receptionist answered.

Placing the call on speaker phone, Kat said, "Well, not today."

The clerk asked, "Is there a problem?"

As Kat relayed her concerns, the clerk could be heard shuffling through paperwork.

"Oh, yes. I see you requested no house-keeping services during your stay. Is that correct?"

Kat answered, "Yes."

The clerk didn't sound disturbed or surprised by the occurrence on the fourth floor. She explained, "The woman seen entering your room… that would be our resident ghost, Theodora."

"I told you it was Theodora!" Nicole exclaimed, thrilled to be vindicated.

"Shhhh!" Kat warned, putting her hand over the phone.

The receptionist continued, "It's believed that Theodora lived at the hotel when it was a cancer clinic. We don't know if she was a patient, a nurse, or housekeeper, but 419 was her room. Guests often report returning to the room to find it neat and organized and their bags packed."

"Seriously, that's what you're going with— Wait, what? A *ghost* cleaned our room?" Kat asked, hanging up the phone with a loud bang.

Mariah felt a deepening dread. *The dead live here. They walk the halls and haunt the rooms of the Crescent Hotel.*

# Chapter 19

"**All** aboard!" the driver yelled from the open door of the green trolley. Mariah and Nicole, last in line, paid the fee and claimed a seat. The ride, a three-mile trek, traveled along Prospect Avenue and down the mountain, giving visitors a taste of what the quaint town had to offer.

Disappointed that Kat couldn't be persuaded to spend the afternoon as a tourist, they left her scouring the hotel's archive wall outside SkyBar. Scribbling notes like a forensic scientist, searching for a lead in some whodunit mystery, Kat absently waved the two on. "I'll catch up with you this evening at the Halloween parade."

Nicole found the trolley a delightful combination of entertainment and transportation. Victorian-style homes being prepped for tricker-treaters peeked through the spectacular display of fall colors along the route.

Passengers chattered, their voices rising and blending as the car traversed curves and zigzagged parked vehicles along the narrow street to downtown Eureka Springs. Taking a right on Spring Street, the trolley slowed.

The heart of the historic town was alive around them. Tourists, shoppers, and sight-seers walked along the pavement outside stores decked out for the fall festivities. Cars, motorcycles, and delivery trucks crawled the avenue, stopping now and then for pedestrians trying to cross to the other side.

As the trolley neared where Mariah and Nicole wanted to get off, Nicole pulled the overhead strap. The *ting-ting* of the trolley bell signaled the driver to stop. The two joined the crowd, walking the pavement on both sides of the street. The town was vibrant, pulsing with a strange energy. The unique downtown artsy vibe and historic surroundings made for a destination unlike anything they had ever experienced.

Mariah and Nicole took in the sights and sounds around them as they window-shopped the blocks of one-of-a-kind gift stores, fine art galleries, and craft emporiums. They stopped occasionally when a display caught their eye but were not tempted to venture inside until coming to a specialty boutique. Oracle & Sage offered numerous services, including tarot, aura, and astrology readings.

Mariah grabbed Nicole's hand and drug her up the wooden steps to an outdoor deck. Nicole tried to break free, but Mariah held firm. "I've always wanted to have an aura reading. Now's my chance, and you are coming with me!"

"Wait!" Nicole insisted, refusing to move one step further. "Aura…?"

Mariah took a moment to come up with an explanation that might tempt Nicole to give it a try. "Some people believe thoughts and emotions create an unseen energy field around a person called an aura. A special camera is used to capture the energy. Different types of energy appear as different colors in the photograph. Each color has its own unique meaning and provides a special insight into a person's emotional and spiritual well-being."

Nicole flashed on her last visit to Eureka Springs with the strange gypsy fortune-teller and the unsettling tarot card reading. She did not hesitate, "Nah, I'll pass."

Mariah stared at Nicole; disappointment plastered across her face. "Okay, I'll get a reading and you can enjoy looking around," she suggested, holding the door for her friend.

The upscale shop was light and airy. The white walls lined with glass shelves filled with books and gifts were much different from the carnival fortune-teller atmosphere Nicole had expected. The all-female staff was polite and appeared to be genuinely caring and interested in helping customers. One was patiently advising an elderly woman on the use of essential oils, while another was helping a young couple find just the right scented candle for their new home.

Mariah stopped at a glass display case filled with a large selection of jewelry and waited for a consultant to schedule an aura photo and reading.

Nicole browsed with no intention of making a purchase. It was the kind of shop she had often wondered about. Tarot and oracle cards, along with figurines and statues, were all neatly stacked on tables or arranged on shelves. Lost in the realm of magic and mysticism, she soon forgot the outside world.

The last of the four rooms was filled with candles and incense. She stepped closer and read the sign posted on the open door.

## The Healing Power of Smudging
Cleansing Rituals to Purify Your Home,
Attract Positive Energy,
and Bring Peace into Your Life.

Intrigued, Nicole surveyed the room. Every available space was packed with natural and organic smudging products, including sage bundles, incense sticks, and scented candles. Nicole picked up a sage kit that claimed to contain everything needed to cleanse a space. Turning the package over, she scanned the directions on the back. *Just what I need.*

On the way to check out, she passed a wooden stand lined with different colored crystals hanging from silver chains. When she leaned in closer to get a better look, the stand began to shake. A blue crystal began to quiver in place and to swing back and forth on its chain as if reaching out to her.

Nicole scooted back from the display and looked around to see if anyone had noticed the strange occurrence.

A staff member raised her eyebrows at Nicole and said, "I think the crystal is speaking to you."

"Well, do you have any idea what it's saying?"

"It wants to go home with you."

"What…?" Nicole began, then stopped mid-sentence, read the sign above the wooden stand, and asked, "What's a dousing pendulum?"

"Think of it as a miniature Ouija board."

Nicole grabbed the chain to the blue crystal and placed it beside the smudging kit at the checkout registrar. Paying, she shoved the purchases into her purse, then waited for Mariah, now seated in front of the aura reader.

"Oh…!" The reader placed a hand over her heart, raising her eyes from the photograph as she looked at Mariah. "Your aura is… indigo, an unusual color between blue and violet."

"Is that good or bad?" Mariah asked, head tilting to the side.

Taking a deep breath and letting it out again slowly, the reader explained, "It's one of the rarest aura colors. It's the color created when a person has very powerful spiritual energy."

"Which means?" Mariah asked.

In a voice meant for Mariah's ears only, the reader said, "Indigo signifies a special connection to the supernatural realm and the afterlife."

The young woman stood and handed

Mariah a folder. "This is your Aura Report. It is an in-depth description on the colors in your aura, who you are, and what is happening in your life."

"I'm pretty sure I know who I am and what is happening in my life, but it might make for an interesting read later." Mariah said. Accepting the folder, she paid for the reading and hurried to locate Nicole.

Leaving the boutique, Nicole asked, "Learn anything you didn't already know?"

"Yep. I learned that I'm unique." Mariah answered.

## Chapter 20

**On** the narrow street, streamers and fake cobwebs fluttered from the rooftops of the century-old buildings. Glowing jack-o-lanterns lit up the sidewalks. Eye-catching displays of black cats, bubbling cauldrons, Grim Reapers, and broken tombstones filled each storefront window. Halloween had arrived!

The historic downtown district was flooded with tourists and locals. The most popular viewing spots along the parade route were already claimed. Nicole and Mariah joined the flow of late arrivals maneuvering lawn chairs, clusters of friends, people in costumes, and parents with children on their shoulders.

Mariah barely caught Nicole's comment over the loud chatter. "Look up, a full moon is rising. The crazies are on the loose." Feeling spooky danger lurking around every corner, she said, "We need to find Kat. I've seen enough scary movies to know that people wearing masks on the night of a full moon are not always friendly.

Anxiety taking a front row seat at the parade, Nicole warned, "We could be walking in the direction of something we should be running away from."

Uneasiness increasing, afraid she might get swallowed up by a lunar-crazed current of warm bodies, Nicole grabbed Mariah's arm. Walking the pace of the swelling crowd, the two moved as if invisible hands dragged them this way and that until they finally caught sight of Kat.

Relieved, Nicole let out a long sigh and waved.

Kat motioned for the latecomers to cross the street where she had staked out a place to view the parade. Making room on the packed sidewalk, she said, "I was about to give up on you two."

Mariah flashed a piercing stare in Kat's direction. "We had to wade through a throng of hundreds to find you, so this had bettered be good."

The blast of a police siren ended the conversation and drew cheers from the spectators as the "Zombie Crawl" began.

Behind the red-and-blue flashing lights, the street filled with hordes of zombies followed by ghouls, creepy clowns, magicians, contortionists, marching bands, and spooky dancers. In the twilight of Halloween night, the street teeming with the undead set the mood for the annual "Thriller" reenactment.

Clapping broke out up and down the avenue. The crowd lining the pavement stood, waving flags and holding up signs. Mariah's attention was drawn to the whistles and shouts from the Basin Park Hotel. She looked up to the second-floor Balcony Bar packed with rowdy customers peering down on the zombie apocalypse. She decided against looking at the third-floor row of windows. After the disastrous stay at the historic hotel last summer, she was not yet ready for round two with spirits from the hotel. Instead, she turned her attention back to the parade and said, "Nothing pays homage to All Hallows' Eve as much as… well… streets swarming with the undead."

"It's as if Hell released all its monsters for this night," Nicole mumbled as the sounds of dragging body parts, hungry growls, and snapping of rotting teeth echoed the length of Spring Street.

"Welcome to Arkansas's scary side," Kat announced as a procession of decaying corpses rocking to "Monster Mash" passed. They moved stiffly and slowly, with their arms outstretched in front. Heads tilted to the side; sunken eyes scanned the sidewalks for their next meal.

"I hate the undead," Nicole declared, spotting an Elvis zombie taking selfies with his wannabe brain donors. "People dressed up like monsters and creeping from one part of a town to another is *not* my idea of a fun Halloween parade," she grumbled, disgusted by the mindless lumbering undead.

"What about skeletons?" Kat asked as the sound of bone hitting asphalt announced the "Dance of the Dead."

A shaft of moonlight hit an army of dancing skeletons on the move. The head of one swiveled, and its coal-black sockets locked on Nicole.

A small yelp escaped from Nicole when one of its skinless arms pointed in her direction.

Noticing Nicole's reaction, Kat decided to tease her. Giggling, she formed a cross with her fingers and stepped between the skeleton and his target.

110

Hissing displeasure, it rejoined the march of the dead.

"Don't be afraid. He can only dance around after dark. When the sun comes up, that bag of bones will return to his grave."

Nicole glared at Kat. Voice shaky, she said, "I do not find that bit of information in the least comforting."

"I swear, you are afraid of your own shadow. What has caused this mental derangement?"

"Oh, let me count the reasons. One—it began when I was six with a game of hide-and-seek. Somehow, I got locked in our bedroom closet and missed trick-or-treating because it took Dad most of the night to break into the dark prison. *I* missed trick-or-treating but, Kat? Oh no, not her. You came home all smiles with a big bag filled to the top with candy. Number two—you booked our yearly girl's getaway vacation last year at the Basin Park Hotel, one of the most haunted hotels in Arkansas. I barely escaped with my sanity." Voice rising, she continued, "Three—this year, I find myself an unwilling guest at the Crescent Hotel where our cleaning lady is dead… dead… dead! And, four—"

Mariah elbowed Kat. Their eyes met.

The condemning stare triggered Kat, and she held up both hands in surrender.

Nicole studied her sister. "You know, there's a name for your pattern of irresponsible behavior—Responsibility Deficit Disorder."

"All right, I may have had something to do with your insecurity problems," Kat admitted. "I'm sorry. If it's any comfort, it's 'treat' time," she said, pointing to floats with crazed zombies imprisoned in cages and post-apocalyptic vehicles generously tossing sweet treats.

Kids waved from the sidewalk, squealing, arms waving, begging, "Throw me something!"

Meanwhile, Zombie hunters walked the sidelines bringing up the rear of the crawl, dressed in gas masks, combat boots, army fatigues, and SWAT tactical gear.

Kat retrieved a handful of skeleton-themed mints. With a smile, she dropped the chocolate candy into her sister's hands as a peace offering and asked, "How about a double shot of nerve medicine at the Voodoo Lounge?"

## Chapter 21

**It** was all-hands-on-deck tending the bar inside the Voodoo Lounge of the New Orleans Hotel. The upscale hot spot was filled with costumed merrymakers. A bartender with rolled-up sleeves moved from one end of the counter to the other. The whirr of a blender could be heard over the laughter and *clink* of ice against glass.

A mirrored wall behind the bar reflected the spirit of the partygoers. On one wall, a television played a Halloween slasher film. Mummies, ghouls, and other beasts of the night stood or sat at the tall, pub-style tables.

The Addam's family claimed the bar seating. In his signature pinstriped suit, Gomez held hands and exchanged kisses with a pale-skinned Morticia in a skin-tight, black hobble gown.

Kat moved smoothly, sidestepping the octopus-like tentacles at the hem. Son

Pugsley and daughter Wednesday stopped their game of tug-of-war over a headless doll to allow the three newcomers to pass.

"We're lucky to get a table," Kat said, claiming the last empty spot. Snagging the server's attention, she ordered drinks.

"Feels like we've invaded forbidden territory," Mariah said, uncomfortable with stares from surrounding tables.

Nicole's eyes were pulled from one table after another, then stopped. In one dark corner, she spotted the skeleton from the parade.

With a lopsided grin, it waved and winked.

"Hm-mmm... monsters to the right of us ... monsters to the left of us ... and here we are stuck in the middle with you. Yep, *real* lucky tonight."

Kat chose to ignore the sarcastic remark. "I like to think of it more as... well... a bag of spooky fun filled with people dressed up, pretending to be magical creatures," she said, admiring the creativity.

"People went all out on their disguises," Nicole commented to the server when he returned with a tray of drinks. "I feel self-conscious showing up maskless," she said, taking a deep drink of the Bloody Mary in front of her.

Kat laughed. "I'd feel uncomfortable, too, if I were you, but not because of being maskless." Pointing to the red concoction piled high with bacon, olives, dill pickles, and okra, she asked, "Is that dinner?"

Munching on the okra, Nicole only replied, "Yum."

Drink tray held high to avoid collisions; their server collected the money. Before moving on, he explained, "Halloween is the one time of year when people can dress up and become whatever they wish."

"A great idea," Kat said, pulling three beautiful, feathered masquerade face masks from the shopping bag she had been guarding all night. Removing her glasses, she replaced them with a mask. "Now we can join the fun and not feel bad about misbehaving."

Nicole pulled on a black sequined cat's-eye mask and wagged a finger. "Just remember, a mask does *not* mean you are no longer accountable for your actions."

"You're not my mother," Kat insisted, shoving the last mask in Mariah's direction.

"No, but the rules our parents taught us

still hold. Rule Number 1: you do the crime, you do the time."

Kat downed the tequila shot, licked the salt from her fist, then bit into the lime. "Since when does having fun qualify as a criminal offense?"

Mariah jiggled the red lace mask until it felt comfortable on her nose, then looked at Kat. "Depends on the one having the fun. Remember the frat party we crashed? Out of control drinking, cops, arrests…"

Green eyes stared across the table to find two pairs of eyes staring back. *So, how do you beat the odds when it's two against one?* Kat wondered. She could stand strong and fight to stay in control… or surrender because, some-times, you're just outnumbered.

Saved from answering by the scraping of a chair along the floor, everyone's attention was drawn to where an extremely tall Dracula stood. Flinging a black cape dramatically over one shoulder, the Vampire King growled through long white fangs.

Eyes blazing, he pointed across the room to a table littered with wooden stakes where Vampire hunter, Van Helsing, sat, slowly spinning a highball glass.

Recognizing the challenge, Helsing

jumped to his feet and flashed a gold crucifix. The two stood toe-to-toe in the center of the crowded room.

Everyone went quiet.

*Trouble brewing in Monsterville*, Nicole observed.

Enjoying the show, Mariah downed her beer and signaled the bartender for another round. "Definitely some bad blood between those night creatures."

A truce was called when a creepy little clown with a wicked smile jumped in between the two mortal enemies. The entire bar broke out in applause and cheers before returning to their drinks.

"See? Misbehaving can be fun," Kat pointed out, feeling vindicated.

Refills on the table, voice low and hushed, Kat leaned close. "Thanks to the Crescent Hotel archives, I have uncovered some interesting facts. On the fourth floor, there's a small museum and library. Many of the books tell the unique history of Eureka Springs, while others tell the story of the Crescent Hotel."

Producing a small spiral notebook from her purse, she opened to the first page of scribbled notes and read, "The history of

Eureka Springs is tied to the history of the natural springs that circle the area. Native Americans considered them sacred. In 1856, Dr. Alvah Jackson claimed that the waters of Basin Spring had cured his son's eye infection. As word spread of the healing waters, the sick flocked to the area. Within a period of years, the tent-covered hillsides went from a campground to rural village to the flourishing resort town it is now."

Turning the page, Kat looked up. Seeing she still had everyone's attention, she continued, "At the time the hotel was built in 1886, it was considered the premiere vacation destination west of the Mississippi. And I found the most interesting information on the outer wall of the library. The hall-length exhibit displayed pictures and newspaper articles memorializing the history of the hotel, and one entire section was dedicated to Norman Baker. It seems the Crescent Hotel closed its doors in 1934, then, in 1937, reopened as Baker's Cancer Clinic."

Mariah interrupted the history lesson. "So, let me see if I have this right. The hotel went from a luxury resort to a hospital?"

Kat nodded, then continued, "Okay, this

is where the story takes a dark turn. The 1930s was the time of the Great Depression. All across America, thousands were out of work and homeless. It was no different in Eureka Springs. The renovation of the hotel and establishment of a hospital provided jobs—good-paying jobs for people in the area. The clinic saved the town. Where, once the sick had flocked to the area for the healing waters, now they came for what came to be known as Baker's Formula #5 Miracle Cure. Baker was hailed a hero for saving the town and for giving the hopeless hope."

Seeing she had the full attention of her listeners, Kat took a long breath, then let it out slowly. "It turns out Baker was no savior or hero. He was a real, living, breathing… monster."

# Chapter 22

**Oblivious** to the car horns, the Crescent Hotel's courtesy van pulled right up to the No Parking section of the street. And with even more disregard, the driver got out and opened the front and back doors. "Good evening, ladies," he said in a gruff voice, nodding in Kat's direction.

Kat read the name tag pinned to the driver's uniform. "Thanks, Benny, for the ride," she said, settling into the front seat while Nicole and Mariah slid into the back.

The van pulled away from the curb. Benny navigated the narrow streets of the historic downtown district without a word. Streetlamps flickered at the van's passing. Leaving behind the shoulder-to-shoulder antique buildings occupied by quaint shops, galleries, and bistros, the van climbed the mountain to the hotel. The driver's white hair was all that could be made out in the dark.

The passengers rode in silence for a few minutes before Nicole said, "Strange that only the Historic Loop leads to the Crescent."

Benny loved talking to his customers and was willing to discuss anything that got them engaged in conversation. With no more than a split-second look at the rearview mirror, he said, "The original roads in Eureka Springs were Native American and animal trails. If you stay on the Historical Loop to the top of Crescent Mountain, you will find that no street crosses it, but, instead, all merge with the Loop and end at the Crescent Hotel."

"I find the winding street confusing. I think it would be easy to get lost and never be found on this mountain," Mariah said.

Benny pointed out the window as the van's headlights swiped the street. "The secret is to follow the red painted curb. It leads tourists straight to the top of the mountain and the hotel."

Traffic began to crawl, allowing carloads of sightseers to admire the festive lawn and porch displays. From shrieking ghouls to maniacal monsters and spooky skeletons, it seemed too much was just enough for the over-the-top Halloween-themed homes.

"Oh, look!" Nicole directed everyone's

attention to one Victorian house decorated with spider webs, bats, and witches. The owners had even gone so far as to design their own spooky lighting system, complete with homemade mist-producing cauldrons. The front lawn was equipped with a sound-activated device to keep passers-byers on their toes.

Benny explained, "The homes on the Loop are famous for their annual Halloween displays. This stretch attracts hundreds of sightseers and trick-or-treaters."

Mariah glanced out the window at the passing Victorian homes. She wasn't interested in the ones all lit up for the night of fun. It was the ones that sat dark and unwelcoming that drew her attention. No lights or decorations, they plainly announced, "Stay away. Trick-or-treaters not welcomed." She scanned the windows for shadows shifting within the shadows for ghosts—watchful… patient… biding their time.

Finding none, her gaze started to move on to the next house when traffic came to a complete stop. A group of little monsters trailed by their parents crossed the street. Running from house-to-house, Mariah heard them threatening tricks if no treats were forth coming. "I remember when a Halloween costume at my house meant an old bedsheet with a couple of blackened holes for eyes."

Kat turned and looked over the seat at Nicole. "Remember the time Mom dressed us each in a white cardboard box with red ribbon bows in our hair? You cried because you wanted to go dressed as Cinderella, but I thought it was the greatest Halloween costume ever. Who knew Mom could be so creative!"

Turning back around to the front, she announced, "I'm so glad I live in a world where there are Octobers. I've always loved the month: the cool air, the smell of pumpkin spice, and the candy. As a kid, I looked forward to dressing up in outlandish costumes. Armed with one simple phrase, 'Trick or Treat,' I could demand people put candy in my bag," Kat said.

"Did we come from the same parents?" Nicole asked.

"Why?"

"You aren't normal."

"In my opinion, being normal is vastly overrated."

Nicole said, "I find Halloween confusing. Our entire childhood, our parents beat Rule

#10 into our heads: never take candy from strangers. And then, for one night a year, they dressed us up in crazy costumes, pushed us out the door, and said, 'Go beg for candy.'"

Put out at Nicole's lack of respect for the fun holiday, Kat said, "And guess what? You survived. Forget that kid stuff. We are involved in a real-life mystery: Norman Baker… Cancer Hospital… strange happenings at the Crescent Hotel."

"Well, I think I have solved that mystery. The hotel is haunted," Nicole shot back.

"Ghosts aren't real," Kat groaned, wishing she could prove to her sister, *normal* was not believing in the spirit world.

Benny liked talkative customers and was enjoying the heated exchange. Chatty passengers made the time pass by quicker. He might even learn something from them or, on rare occasions, teach them something. "What room are you ladies staying in?"

"419," the three passengers answered in unison.

"Theodora's room," Nicole whispered, voice shaky.

"Oh, so you've met Theodora. She's quite the trickster, tidying up for guests when they leave the room.

"Let's just say that she made her presence known," Mariah explained.

Nicole filled in the details. "She folded our clothes, packed our bags, and arranged some of the things we had left scattered around the room."

"You'll never convince me it wasn't housekeeping," Kat insisted.

Ignoring her friend's outburst, Mariah thought it might be useful information to know which other rooms were infested with ghosts, so they could stay clear of them. "What's the most requested room?" she asked.

"Room 218. Michael's room."

Nicole jumped in, "What's his story?"

Kat rummaged in her purse, locating notebook and pencil, ready to jot down any relevant information.

"Michael is the most legendary of all the hotel's ghosts. He was an Irish stonemason working on the construction of the hotel in 1884. A good-looking young man, he loved the ladies. It's believed he was flirting with a passing woman when he fell to his death, landing in room 218. If ghosts are your thing, book that room next time."

"Why?" Mariah asked, making a mental note of the room number.

"The room is most active when occupied by women. Michael is full of mischief then: running water, opening and closing doors, and turning lights off and on."

A die-hard skeptic, Kat said, "I'm having trouble sifting through the imagined to find the real among these stories."

Benny quickly glanced at the front seat passenger. "You aren't the only one. When the present owners purchased the Crescent Hotel in 1997, the resort already had the reputation of being America's most haunted hotel. They inherited a confusing hotel history, intertwined with a hundred years' worth of ghost stories. Over the years, they have allowed mediums and ghost hunters to investigate the building and property in an effort to piece together the hotel's true story."

"So, what was the verdict?" Mariah asked, knowing from experience with Morris the cat that some of the stories were real.

"Water plus limestone equals paranormal activity. Eureka Springs is surrounded by water. Crescent Mountain, the hilltop the hotel sits on, is predominantly limestone. The hotel is completely built from limestone blocks."

The van pulled up in front of the hotel.

Benny jumped out, opened the doors, and suggested, "The findings of the ghost hunters, plus the startling number of repeated sightings recorded over the decades, became the basis of what has become the nightly Crescent Hotel Ghost and Morgue Tours. If you want to find out about the hauntings, take the ghost tour. If you want to learn more about Dr. Baker and the Cancer Clinic, I suggest you take the Morgue Tour."

## Chapter 23

**Nicole** waved to Kat and Mariah, who had decided to take Benny up on his suggestion of the Morgue Tour. Nicole wanted no part of it. Running through the shadows, chasing after rumors and reports of ghosts was more than a curiosity with her sister; it was an addiction.

From their last confrontation, Nicole had learned a very valuable lesson: steer clear of discussions about the supernatural. When it came to debunking stories of paranormal activity, her sister was like a dog with a bone, stubborn and relentless. She had an answer for every question.

During the heated argument, Nicole had asked, "What about ghost-hunting TV shows, people using scientific equipment to record or measure spirit activity?"

Kat had answered, "The creepy photos and videos make it seem like ghosts exist.

However, none of this offers good evidence of ghosts. Some are hoaxes created to fool people. The rest only prove that equipment can sometimes capture noise, images, or other signals that people don't expect. Ghosts are the least-likely explanation."

"What about people who report ghosts doing things that scientists say are impossible, such as becoming invisible or passing through walls?"

"Scientists, using reliable research methods, have found zero evidence that ghosts exist. What scientists have discovered, though, is that you can't always trust your eyes, ears, or brain."

"How do they explain the phenomena then?"

"Dreaming with your eyes wide-open."

Realizing she could not argue with insanity, Nicole had thrown her hands in the air.

As she'd walked away, Kat had yelled at her back, "Why are ghosts terrible liars?" Not waiting for a reply, she said, "Because you can see right through them."

The crazy fit of laughing that had followed had Nicole thinking, *Maybe it's time for some sort of intervention or rehab for Kat.*

Weaving in and out of the lobby traffic, she arrived at the base of the back stairs, a shortcut. She ran her hand along the smooth, slightly rounded banister as she climbed. Giving access to all floors at the north end of the hotel, the narrow steps swept upward.

Reaching the first-floor landing, she found a couple taking pictures with their cell phones. She walked around them to the next flight of stairs.

On the second floor, a girl around twelve years old played outside a room while two young girls watched from the unmade bed. The girl took turns kicking different-sized balls to the end of the hall and watching them roll back.

A voice from the room yelled, "Sarah, get back in here and close the door!"

Ignoring the order, Sarah continued the game. When the woman appeared at the door, the girl scurried to collect the balls. Seeing Nicole, the woman explained, "We took the ghost tour the first night of our stay, and now all they want to do is play with Breckie."

Confused, Nicole asked, "Breckie?"

"Well, it seems the Crescent was once a

college, and the son of the school's president, four-year-old Breckie—"

"Mom, his name is Clifton Breckinridge Thompson." The youngest girl climbed down from the bed, came to the door, and looked up. "Mommy, his nickname was Breckie."

"Thank you honey. Clifton, AKA Breckie, died of complications from appendicitis. The tour guide said he still bounces his ball in the hallways, and the second floor is his favorite hangout."

The third girl joined her sister at the door, "He's got curly blond hair, and wears weird clothes, and he played ball with us last night."

Shushing her daughter, the woman pushed the three back into the room. "It's no secret that my kids have rampant imaginations. It's one of our favorite things about them."

Before shutting the door, she explained, "Nothing screams 'Happy Halloween' as much as a door opening from a gust of wind or floorboards creaking in an empty room. Things always seem a bit creepier come October. But when your kiddos swear they have seen a spirit… Now, *that's* scary."

Nicole just smiled, not knowing how to respond. As a self-professed chicken and proud scaredy cat, she was willing to entertain the question of whether or not ghosts really exist. But had the three sisters really seen an apparition or was it just wishful thinking? No way to tell with kids. Ask a kid if they believe in Santa Claus on December 23, and the answer will probably be *yes* because they want to believe around Christmas time. Ask a kid if ghosts are real around Halloween and the answer will probably be *yes* because, again, they want to believe.

Nicole walked around the wall and peered up the next set of stairs. She took the first step, then another, then another. It felt unnaturally still; the only sounds she could hear were her own breathing and the soft creaking beneath her feet.

She paused halfway up. Something wasn't right. The silence had become oppressive and the air heavy as if before a storm, almost suffocating.

She took a shaky step; heart beating faster as she clung to the handrail with a white-knuckled grip. She couldn't shake the feeling she was being watched. Nicole quickly looked over her shoulder down the way she had come.

Nothing.

She wiped a bead of sweat from her forehead with a quivering hand, then took another step.

The old staircase moaned with every footfall. Determined not to let her fears overcome reason, Nicole gave herself a mental shake. *You're not a child. Stop letting your imagination rule your emotions.*

# Chapter 24

**The** third-floor hallway was blocked by a group of ghost hunters. No way around; Nicole decided against plowing straight through and interrupting the tour guide's story. Instead, she listened to it.

"The 1886 Crescent Hotel has the reputation of being America's most haunted hotel. Floor by floor, you learned about the most active spirits, from Dr. John Freemont Ellis, the house physician, known for being a heavy pipe smoker of cherry tobacco, to the children who appear as poltergeists.

"One of the resort's most infamous eras was from 1937 to 1940. The Crescent Hotel had been sold to Norman Baker, a radio personality known for criticizing big business and the American Medical Association. Baker renovated the building and turned it into a cancer hospital.

"Although Baker, a high school dropout,

hadn't spent a day in any sort of medical training, he claimed to have an alternative treatment for cancer. Despite glowing advertisements promoting the miracle cure, many people died under his care."

The guide drew everyone's attention to the north end of the hall. "Baker did not believe in using painkillers. Patients in late stages of cancer were moved to a soundproof wing of the hospital Baker had added when he took over the resort. Behind locked doors, no one could witness their suffering or hear their screams."

A young man with purple-streaked hair and a nose ring at the back of the group asked, "And when they died, what happened?"

"Nurses rolled their bodies down to the morgue on gurneys in the middle of the night.

Once on the autopsy table, Baker removed tumors and healthy tissue from the deceased. He then placed the body parts in jars of his secret formula for examination and further study."

Just outside the annex entrance, Nicole noticed a man reach for a woman within the tour group who had suddenly turned pale and fallen against the wall.

Hand to her forehead, she said, "I feel dizzy."

As the woman plopped onto one of the two chairs always kept near the annex entrance for just such occurrences, the tour guide reassured the onlookers, "Nothing to worry about. She'll be okay. Every so often, someone feels faint or ill in this area. Most people recover within minutes, if not immediately."

What was revealed next chilled Nicole to the core.

"This spot on the third floor is believed to be a 'portal to the other side' or a dimension that holds the spirits of the dead. The portal is directly above the hotel basement where the notorious Baker morgue was located. A medium who investigated the hotel believes the portal and the morgue have a supernatural connection."

Excited tourgoers began snapping photos, aiming cell phones indiscriminately at the walls, the floors, the lighting fixtures. The paranormal bug had bitten; the cure was photographic evidence of paranormal activity—a dark, shadowy figure against a wall, a whisp of white mist floating overhead, a translucent human form walking the hall.

"I'm out of here," Nicole whispered to herself, scrambling away from the group and up the stairs to the fourth floor. Having a ghostly encounter at a historic landmark made for a great story and could be a thrilling experience for some, but not for Nicole. She knew from staying at the Basin Park Hotel, Crescent's sister hotel, how quickly things could go from fun to spooky to downright scary.

## Chapter 25

**On** the last rung of stairs, muffled voices from below drifted upward, then died away slowly. In the intense silence that followed, Nicole caught herself longing for the safety of the cozy two-story home she had left behind in Missouri. She paused at the fourth-floor landing, looking over her shoulder to ensure she hadn't been followed, then made a dash for room 419.

A wave of nervousness overtook her at the entrance. She fumbled a long time with the key before it fit into the lock. The rattling of the metal against metal was the only sound in the narrow corridor. At last, with one loud *click*, the key turned. With a backward glance, Nicole went in quickly, then slammed the door behind her.

Catching her breath, Nicole leaned against the door. Eyes closed, she struggled to get control. Wrangling in her emotions, she walked to the center of the sitting room and conducted a full 360-degree surveillance. No whispers from the dark, no flickering lights, no fleeting shadows.

*Now what?* she wondered. Her brain scrambled for an answer, then a lightbulb went off in her head. *Best way to handle a problem is to consult the experts.*

Groping parade candy and cell phone from a pant pocket, Nicole sat cross-legged on the nearest wingback chair. Dropping her purse onto the coffee table, then popping a chocolate into her mouth, Nicole switched on her cell phone.

Luckily, rituals for removing unwanted spirits abounded on the internet.

After scrolling for several minutes, she came across the headline, "What To Do If You Think You Have A Ghost." Clicking on the site, she found four simple steps for getting rid of uninvited guests of the paranormal kind.

Step 1: Communicate with a dowsing pendulum. Nicole read the directions and then dug the crystal she had purchased at Oracle & Sage from her purse. It appeared that the pendulum could only be used to answer *yes* or *no* questions. If the question was *yes*, the pendulum would swing clockwise. If the answer was *no*, it would swing counterclockwise.

Nicole grasped the end of the chain with her right hand, allowing the crystal to hang loose above her left palm. When the pendulum stopped moving, she ask the question, "What is yes?" She watched as the crystal quivered over the center of her outstretched hand and then began to swing clockwise.

"Whoa!" Nicole yelped, dropping the pendulum like a hot potato. Eyes circling the room, she searched for anything out of place.

Seeing nothing, she gathered her courage and picked the crystal off the floor. She couldn't chicken out now. She needed some answers before she could rid the room of any unwelcome visitors.

Placing the pendulum over her palm again, she asked the first of two questions. "Is there a spirit in the room?" The crystal quivered, then began to swing clockwise, then stopped. As it swept across her palm, she felt a flow of energy between the point of the stone and her skin as if a magnetic force field had been created.

Not surprised by the answer, Nicole asked, "Is your name Theodora?" When the pendulum swung "yes," she had her answer.

Finished with the interrogation, Nicole followed the last direction for speaking with spirits. Holding tightly to the silver-chained pendulum, she said, "Goodbye, Theodora," ending the communication with the spirit.

Nicole took a deep breath and leaned back in the chair. She whispered, "So far, so good." Gathering her thoughts, Nicole rested her head on one of the cushions for a moment, then sat up, ready for Step 2: Cleansing the space of spirits.

Uncurling from the chair, Nicole stood and stretched. She snatched a complimentary bottle of water from beside the coffee maker and sipped from it while reviewing the instructions for her next move. She returned to the chair, then stacked the remaining ghost-sanitizing supplies from Oracle & Sage on the coffee table: a box of kosher salt, matches, abalone shell, feather, and smudge bundle.

Before lighting the five-inch-long pack of sticks, she cracked the door, the only escape route for Theodora. After burning for a few seconds, the flame went out on its own.

Brown smoke swirled and drifted upward, filling the air with a woodsy perfume. Holding the bundle over the shell to catch any ashes, she circled the room fanning the smoke with the feather. Making sure to smudge each room, she did as the directions said, paying special attention to any outward-facing corners. Apparently, corners act as boundaries between the space being cleansed and the spirit world.

To make certain Theodora had vacated the suite, Nicole took out the crystal and asked the last question. "Is there a spirit in the room?" The crystal quivered and she once again felt the strange magnetic pull between the stone and her palm.

Holding her breath, she waited, counting, "One second… two seconds… three seconds…" The stone went still.

No answer so it was safe to proceed with the cleansing. The last thing she wanted was to be locked in the room with a cranky spirit.

Fired up and ready to finish the job, Nicole skimmed Step 3: Salting. She was surprised to learn ghosts hated the white mineral. It had the power to put some sort of whammy on them.

Nicole closed the entrance door and

then grabbed the box of salt. She poured a half-inch wide white line along the floor under the front door, on the windowsills, and the fireplace, creating a protective boundary. Unable to cross a salt line, the spirit of Theodora was now locked out of the space she loved to haunt. For good measures, Nicole tossed a handful of salt into each air vent.

She circled the sitting room and then peeked into the bedroom and bathroom. The air felt lighter, fresher… inviting. With a smile that stretched from ear to ear, Nicole brushed her hands together and declared, "Problem solved!"

# Chapter 26

**The** hotel filled with late-night laughter and chatter. Bellhops maneuvered luggage carts for late arrivals. Fun-loving couples waited at the elevator for a ride to the SkyBar. Further down the hall, a wedding celebration poured from the glass-walled conservatory.

In the bustling lobby, a group gathered at the concierge desk—a curious hexagonal affair. A young woman in Victorian attire introduce herself. "My name is Jill, and I will be your tour guide tonight." Responsible for entertaining the guests for the next forty-five minutes, Jill began her performance. "Halloween is upon us, but for fans of spooky ghost stories, the haunting season never has to end. To experience spine-tingling chills at any time, simply book a room at a historic hotel."

Collecting tickets, she continued, "There have been more than three hundred hotels inducted into Historic Hotels of America since it was founded in 1989. While hundreds visit these resorts each year, it's rumored that some guests check in… but never check out. Even so, none of the ghost tales can rival the ones from the history of the Crescent Hotel, which might have been taken straight from one of Steven King's horror novels."

Making a grand gesture of opening the French doors to the sweeping East balcony, Jill welcomed everyone. "Ladies and gentlemen, this is where your journey into the "Twilight Zone" begins. She greeted members as they passed. "Where are you folks from? Is this your first visit to Eureka Springs? Enjoying your stay?"

Two older women in black, distressed ball caps with, "I'm Here for the Boos," embroidered in orange on the front were the first through the doors, followed by several married couples and small groups of friends. A father and mother herded two young boys, both in "Ghosts Live Here" T-shirts over the threshold, corralling them near the iron railing. Kat and Mariah were the last to pass before the doors swung shut.

Checking her watch and counting heads, the tour guide took up a position in front of the group. Anticipating questions, she decided to clear up any confusion. "There are two hotel tours. The Room Tour explores the most active spaces on each floor of the hotel. This is the Morgue Tour. We will delve into the legend of Norman Baker as we investigate the morgue."

Taking the staircase to the Fountain Garden, Jill began her ghost tales. "Over the years, many guests have reported experiencing the unexplainable in the garden." Jill pointed to the black-winged shapes above the hotel, causing everyone to look up. "During a full moon, they can be seen circling the three chimney stacks from dusk to dawn."

"What are they?" the father of the young boys asked.

"Bats," Jill answered.

She then directed everyone's attention to the domed structure just below the hotel. "St. Elizabeth Church is reported to bear a resemblance to a cathedral built sometime in the sixth century A.D. in what was once the city of Constantinople. Some say the sounds of the bells are pure magic, and many have claimed to find peace when entering the limestone chapel. Others report having a more… unsettling experience."

She explained, "As you walk down the stairs below the Crescent and pass through the church bell tower, you will come to a beautiful garden where some guests have reported seeing a young girl sitting on one of the cement benches. When they approach, the girl says she is lost and can't find her parents. Concerned, the guests often go for help or conduct a quick search. Upon returning, they are stunned to find the girl has vanished."

"Oh, boy. We need to keep Nicole away from the church and that story," Mariah whispered to her friend.

Kat nodded. "That's all we need… stories of a kiddie ghost now that she is finally finding closure after a year of mourning."

"Especially since you would be responsible for her relapse," Mariah said.

Kat reminded her friend, "Hey, the kidnapping, reservations at the most haunted hotel in America, and attending a Zombie invasion were all decisions sanctioned by both of us. We share the responsibility and any consequences."

"And your baby sister will seek quick and lethal retribution if this girl's getaway is a repeat of our last trip to Eureka Springs— Basin Park Hotel and the ghost cowboy."

Kat thought for a moment, then said, "Yeah, you're right."

Mariah winched just thinking about the possibilities. "She would feel justified stuffing our bodies in the trunk of her car and then helping the police look for us."

Locking eyes in agreement, pinky-swearing to keep the kiddie ghost a secret, the two refocused their attention on the tour guide.

"If you are brave enough to explore the grounds late at night, you might just see the shadowy figure of a tall man walking straight and stiff on one of the moonlight paths."

Hair went up on the back of Mariah's neck as she caught movement out of the corner of her eye. Something shifted in the shadows of the hotel. She tracked the dark shape as it disappeared behind a tree, then reappeared on the other side of the fountain before vanishing from sight. She looked to see if anyone around her had noticed the shadow figure, but everyone was intent on sucking up every sordid detail of the paranormal the guide shared.

"One of our most intriguing ghost stories begins and ends in this very spot. Over the years, many couples have reported having their romantic moonlight stroll interrupted by a young woman falling in a cloud of mist from the third-floor balcony and disappearing before landing where we are standing," Jill said, causing several people to back away. Others frantically dug for their phones and began clicking pictures.

*A-ha… girl in the mist… mystery solved. That explains what I saw on the midnight stroll with my new best friend, Morris*, Mariah told herself.

Kat asked, "Who was the girl? Why did she jump?"

"Those are all good questions, but I'm sorry to say I have no answers for you. Many of the paranormal occurrences reported by guests are linked to real events that occurred at the hotel or involve real people who stayed here. Unfortunately, there is no record of this event ever taking place at the hotel."

Kat lowered her voice and leaned close to Mariah, "I think Rule #75 my mom threatened me with on multiple occasions says it best: *Two can keep a secret if one of them is dead*."

"Shhhh," Mariah hissed, not wanting to miss the ending to the story.

"Even though there is no documented

proof of a young girl falling from the hotel, many believe it is connected to the time in the 1900s when the hotel was the Crescent College Conservatory, a boarding school for girls.

"There are whispers that the young girl was pregnant. Unwed and with child during the Victorian era left women with extremely limited choices; for many, there was only one possible alternative. Was it an accident? Did she jump? Or was she pushed? We will never know," the guide finished.

One thing was certain, Mariah told herself, *The hotel has a past marred by dark secrets… secrets it guards… hidden from those that would pry.*

# Chapter 27

**Mariah** shivered as a sharp wind swept the Ozark Mountain top, scattering leaves. Hunching her shoulders against the chill, she zipped her nylon jacket. She had an uneasy feeling, but what could she do about it now? Deciding the answer was *nothing*, Mariah fell in behind Jill who was leading the way back to the lobby through the glass-paned front doors, then on to the morgue.

The dimly lit path wound around the north side of the hotel, down an incline, guarded by giant oak trees, to a metal annex. Jill pushed the sliding steel door open.

Kat and Mariah entered first, following a corrugated tin hallway that led to a black wooden door. Eyeing the sign, they stopped. Mariah swatted at Kat's hand before she could grab the handle.

"What?"

"Don't you think the picture of a ginormous

human skull tacked to the entrance should be taken as a warning?" Mariah asked, nervous about what they might find once on the other side.

"Warning?"

"Yes. Did it ever enter that head of yours that the past may want to stay buried in the past?"

"By *past*, I assume you mean spirits who have passed from this world to the next? You know my opinion on the paranormal—mind tricks. Ghost hunters see what they want to see, hear what they want to hear, and feel what they want to feel. It's a medical condition—paranormal derangement syndrome."

Ignoring her friend's danger alert, Kat opened the door, then stood back for all who dared to enter.

None refused.

Kat laughed at Mariah's hesitation. Grabbing her friend's hand, she pulled Mariah across the threshold, then closed the door.

Jill waited as the guests scrambled to claim the last of the metal chairs. Mariah guided Kat to an empty spot in the middle of the seating. A device the size of a cell phone, on one of the two empty chairs, started beeping and flashing.

Mariah stopped. "I'm not sitting on a ghost."

Kat looked over Mariah's shoulder. "A ghost?"

Nodding toward the flashing gadget, Mariah explained, "That's an EMF meter. The device is a key part of every paranormal investigation. It detects electrical emissions given off by nearby spirits."

"No, an EMF meter measures AC electromagnetic fields, which are emitted from man-made sources such as electrical wiring… not ghosts," Kat corrected.

With a sigh loud enough to be heard by everyone, Kat squeezed around her friend and picked up the meter. Sitting, she said, "These are the only seats left." She passed the EMF meter to Mariah, and the activity ceased.

Jill caught part of the exchange. Good at reading people, she sensed the two had differing attitudes about the plausibility of the paranormal. One believed; the other did not. She was not concerned. A slight smile tugged at the corners of her mouth because the morgue had an interesting way of dealing with skeptics.

Jill launched her introduction. "Hundreds of people visit the Crescent Hotel each year for one thing—ghost stories. Many think hauntings are common in locations where extreme tragedy has occurred. It's believed the long list of past mishaps at the Crescent is what has opened the door for paranormal activity."

Scanning the excited faces, hungry for more, she continued, "It's the stories that have made our ghost tours so popular. Believers and non-believers alike can come together and have fun exploring the dark history of the hotel."

She paused and pointed to the pictures, signs, and advertisements decorating every wall of the room. "The real horror story centers around Norman Baker and his cancer clinic. In the early 1900s, Eureka Springs relied heavily on tourism. In 1929, the stock market crashed, and the Great Depression followed. People faced many challenges as businesses shut down and banks collapsed. Millions of people found themselves unemployed and homeless."

A woman in the front row blurted out, "My grandparents told me it was a terrible time. Kicked out of their homes… no money…

without jobs, people-built shelters under bridges and even in city dumps."

One of the young boys raised his hand. "We studied about this in history class. My teacher called 'em shanty towns."

Jill listened. When no one else volunteered to share, she said. "In 1934, tough economic conditions caused the Crescent Hotel to close, leaving many of the town's people without jobs. In 1937, the hotel was purchased by millionaire Norman Baker with plans to turn the resort into a sanitarium. His promise of a steady stream of visitors and money was just what the town needed to get back on its feet. Baker was welcomed with a lavish dinner party hosted by city officials with the mayor acting as the emcee."

Jill paused for dramatic effect, then continued, "Baker was a fraud, con artist, and charlatan… and, considered by some to be a serial killer. His secret concoction, which Baker called Formula #5, was a popular treatment even though it was never proven to cure even one case of cancer. It's estimated that the clinic brought in thousands of dollars a year which he squirreled away in various safety deposit accounts known only to him and his assistant, Thelma Yount."

Motioning everyone to follow, Jill led the way to what she called, "The Bottle Display Room." Mariah chose a spot next to wooden shelves stacked with an assortment of old glass containers. Kat moved across the room to lean against a locked metal cabinet. Others headed to the back, where a wooden wheelchair and a skeleton took up most of the space. Huddled together, members of the tour grabbed hold of whoever they had brought along.

"Any ghosts hang out in this room?" Kat asked.

Once everyone was crowded inside, the tour guide answered the question, setting off a flurry of selfies. "Yes. Right where you're standing, a full-bodied apparition was caught on camera by a recent ghost-hunters' TV show. When the episode aired in 2005, it sparked a wave of interest from paranormal enthusiasts. Now, around thirty thousand people take a ghost tour at the hotel each year."

Positioning herself in front of the shelving, Jill resumed the Baker story. "There has been a substantial increase in paranormal activity in the morgue since the 2019 uncovering of a secret bottle grave buried behind the hotel. An archaeologist dug hundreds of bottles from the deep hole. It was determined that the jars contained Baker's secret formula, as well as bits of flesh that had been surgically removed from patients. Many were displayed in the lobby of the hotel when it was the hospital. This exhibit is just a small sample of what was unearthed."

Mariah found something moving about the display. She ran her hand along rows of jars filled with human samples. Some unspoiled by decades underground, she could clearly see specimens floating in a clear liquid. Others were in different stages of deterioration, the rubber seals were cracked, and the body tissue floated in liquid ranging from yellow to black. Fear, pain, and loss radiated from each bottle. Overwhelmed with sadness, Mariah backed away. Feeling the despair of the souls who had passed under the fake doctor's care she thought, *Baker was a monster cloaked in the skin of a healer, selling hope to the hopeless.*

## Chapter 28

**Kat** shuddered. She didn't believe in ghosts, but, if they did exist, she was certain this was where they would be found. The low-ceilinged morgue smelled of dust and dampness. The only light came from a couple of hanging bulbs. The room was empty except for the metal kitchen counter and sink. The farther in she ventured, the cooler it got.

A moment after letting the last guest squeeze into the space, Jill said, "Nurses and patients from Baker's Cancer Cure Hospital are rumored to walk the halls and haunt the rooms of the Crescent Hotel, but it's the morgue that draws the attention of many amateur and professional paranormal investigators."

Scanning the faces and making eye contact with a few, she continued, "Dr. Norman Baker promised his miracle formula was a pain-free cure for cancer in three to six weeks. People flocked to the hospital. Regardless of the diagnosis, the treatments were the same: fresh air, a healthy diet, and injections with one of his secret formulas four to seven times a day.

Because the cure was touted as a pain-free treatment, Baker did not provide pain management for the people in his care. As patients grew worse, they were declared cured and sent home or locked away in the soundproof psychiatric ward where they died a painful death. At this point, the hotel staff would take the patient's pre-signed letter, send it off to the family, and request money for burial arrangements that never happened."

"Oh, those poor people!" an older woman exclaimed, shaking her head. Not understanding the cruelty of some people, she asked, "Why did Baker do this?"

"Greed!" Kat answered for the tour guide.

Jill took back control of the narrative. "Despite Baker's claims that no one ever died in his care, during the three years the cancer hospital was in operation, it's recorded that 44 patients *did* die at the hospital. The dead were moved to the basement and stored in a freezer until they could secretly be spirited away to a crematorium in town."

Jill halted the history lesson. "Feel free to take pictures. You might just capture an image of the dark figure seen recently in this area or an orb."

Cell phones clicked all around in different directions. A young woman near Kat used her phone to record a video of the room. Looking surprised, she pushed play and shoved the screen at Kat. A light spot had been captured zipping across the room. "Is this a reflection or an orb?"

"Or the energy essence of a ghost?" Kat teased. "I don't know, but there is definitely something there."

Jill opened a metal door to a small room, drawing everyone's attention. "The refrigerator room is the last stop on the ghost tour. It's where bodies were stored while waiting for the hearse from the local funeral home." As with each tour, Jill asked, "Anyone want to enter the infamous icebox?"

Kat dragged Mariah to the front and pulled her into the space that had once housed the bodies of the dead. The door closed behind, leaving the two in total darkness.

"Now what?" Mariah asked.

"You still have that EMF meter?"

"Oh, the trusty ghost detector? I thought it might come in handy," Mariah answered, holding up the device and placing it on the floor at Kat's feet. Within seconds, the gadget went crazy, beeping and flashing. She said, "If there's a spirit in this room, please make the meter slow down." The meter slowed immediately. Mariah picked it up.

"Again," Kat urged.

"Thought you didn't believe in ghosts?"

"I don't during the daytime, but, at night, trapped in a walk-in cooler that once stored cadavers, I'm open to reconsidering my—"

Before Kat could finish, the meter in Mariah's hand went wild, flashing and beeping. Startled, she exchanged glances with Kat.

"Do it again!" Kat insisted.

Mariah stared at the meter and concentrated. "If you were a patient at the Baker Cancer clinic, please make the meter slow down." The meter slowed, and, after a few seconds, went silent.

For a moment, the two held their breath. Then, from all around, came a knocking on the walls.

"What's that?" Kat asked, trying to keep the panic from her voice as the knocking turned to pounding.

"Sounds like someone or something trapped in here wants to get out."

Kat and Mariah both rushed to the door at the same time and started banging. Within moments, it opened, and the two, pale and wide-eyed, staggered out.

## Chapter 29

Draped in shadows, the broad, carpeted stair-case rose from the lobby to the fourth floor before them. From the moment they left the morgue, Kat and Nicole were conscious that something followed them. When they went faster, it was left behind, and when they went slower, it caught up. But never once did they look behind themselves, and at each turn in the staircase, they lowered their eyes for fear of what they might see on the stairs above.

Kat hesitated before the second-floor landing, fearful of what waited. In front, the hall stretched into a long, dark passage. Finding it silent and deserted, she signaled Mariah to follow her.

The two had not gone more than a dozen steps when they simultaneously stopped to listen. Kat stepped close in front of Mariah and placed a finger to her lips. "Be quiet," she urged. "There's something here. I heard it."

At that moment, the sound of heavy feet

moving fast along the passage could be heard. Two sets of eyes swept the shadowy hall. Kat uttered a little cry, and, nearly losing her balance, she grabbed for Mariah.

Facing them, directly in their way between the stairs and the elevator, appeared the figure of a man in a dark suit, smoking a pipe. White as death, he stood motionless for the space of a single second. Then he turned and entered room 218…

Without opening the door.

The clamor in Kat's head shrieked, *What's happening here?* She tried to ignore it, but a rush of intense anxiety took hold. In a voice that sounded like someone else's and was only half under control—she urged, "Let's get out of here!"

The smell of cherry tobacco chased after Kat and Mariah as they took the stairs two at a time, never daring to look back. They hesitated, but only for a moment, on the third floor. On high alert, they checked to make sure the coast was clear before venturing down the corridor toward the next set of stairs.

Mariah turned her head and looked where she fancied hearing something moving. *No, nothing. Utter silence. Nothing moved.* Dismissing it, she kept going. But within a few seconds, the sound came again, only louder and closer… wobble, squeak, wobble, squeak.

This time both Mariah and Kat heard the eerie sound. Kat looked into Mariah's eyes with apprehension. They had just enough time to flatten themselves against the wall before a ghostly nurse appeared, wheeling a sheet-draped gurney. The overhead lights flickered, and the nurse and gurney were replaced with empty darkness.

Kat uttered a piercing scream, which Mariah instantly tried to stifle by placing a hand over her friend's mouth. For a second, they stood stock-still, catching their breath.

Not wanting to draw the attention of any other creatures lurking in the dark, Kat asked softly, "Any tips for warding off spirits of the dead?"

Kat felt as if her spine had suddenly become filled with splinters of ice when a voice at her elbow whispered, "Yes… RUN!"

## Chapter 30

**Kat** stood next to Mariah. In front, the fourth floor stretched into a long, dimly lit passage. Shadows filtered noiselessly along the door-lined corridor. Trembling like a leaf, a little voice in her head whispered, *This is made for ghosts.*

Low and shaky, Mariah advised, "Keep your eyes down. Don't look behind us. Don't stop for anything until we cross the finish line." Not taking her eyes off the wall at the far end of the hall, she said, "On my count of three. One…two…three. Go!"

Kat was first out of the gate, with Mariah close behind. Concentrating on the thud of their feet hitting the carpet, Mariah made a beeline for the end of the hall. Kat, imagining something at their backs, waiting for an opportunity, pumped her legs faster. Making a right turn at the end of the hall to room 419, she held both hands up in victory just before hitting door 502 head-on.

*Bam!* Down she went. The door, opening outward into the hall, had once again not been closed.

Stunned for a moment, Kat finally stood and brushed herself off. Before closing the door, the number caught her eye. She turned to Mariah and asked, "Doesn't it seem odd that a door on the fourth floor would be numbered 502?"

Cautious after what they had already experienced at the hands of the hotel, Kat and Mariah snuck a peek around the door. No fleeting shadows, no ghostly presence, only a wooden set of stairs to what appeared to be a room on the next floor.

Mariah said, "Answers the room number question, but doesn't solve the mystery of the open door."

Kat massaged a tender spot on her head while patting down pockets for the key. "I've had it! I'm calling the front desk!" She made eye contact with Mariah." Do not, I repeat, *do not* say anything to Nicole about our…"

Mariah finished the sentence with raised eyebrows, "Misadventures."

"Right." Kat took a deep breath, put on her best happy face, then opened the door.

Nicole, curled up on the couch, looked up from her book, and smiled.

Mariah paused before crossing the threshold. *There is nothing more dangerous than a smiling woman… especially one named Nicole. What has she been up to while we were being hunted by hotel monsters?*

The crunching beneath her feet caused Mariah to look down. When the scent of sage hit, she looked into the eyes of Nicole. They both imagined what the other was thinking.

*I know what you've been up to, Nicole.*

*Please, don't tell on me.*

Breaking eye contact, Mariah entered the room and sat across from Nicole, crossing her arms. The two conspirators focused on Kat, who was circling the room, peeking into every corner.

"What have you been doing?" Kat asked, flashing a fake smile.

Nicole held up the book. "Reading," she answered, unwilling to look her sister in the eye.

Throat dry, Kat tried out the one-cup coffee maker. Pouring in the water, she hit the brew button.

"How was the morgue tour?" Nicole asked, twirling a few strands of hair that had escaped the ponytail.

Kat's mind raced. No way was she going

to tell her sister the truth about the last couple of hours. Stalling, she added powdered creamer to the cup. Running the black plastic stir stick round and round, she scrambled for an answer to the question. Sitting on the couch beside Nicole, she tucked her feet to the side.

"Interesting. The tour guide was an expert historian."

Mariah watched the two sisters dance around the truth. She was not a fan of slippery lies. It was too hard to keep your footing with one because lies had a nasty habit of multiplying. She put the skids on the slippery slide. "When you go hunting for ghosts, they will find you."

Kat slammed her coffee down so hard that it slopped onto the tabletop. *Well, so much for spinning the truth*, the angry voice inside Kat's head said as she swung her legs to the floor and stood. Auburn hair blazing angrily around her face, green eyes sparking fire, nostrils wide, she glared at Mariah.

Seeing the anger bubbling up like a volcano, Mariah advised, "You need to give up on hunting ghosts."

Frustrated, Kat threw up her hands. "I'm searching for a rational explanation, not ghosts. Besides, I can't give up now. it's the looking, not the finding, that's fun," Kat explained, finally admitting the truth.

The room went quiet, each deep in their own thoughts until an odd, half-laugh drifted down from the room above.

All eyes turned upward.

The laughter was replaced by creaking boards and heavy footsteps, pacing back-and-forth, then changed to fierce scratching like a pair of wild animals trying to dig their way through the ceiling.

Feet moving, Kat marched to the bedside phone. Not wanting her anger to get out of control, she took a couple of seconds to put together her thoughts before dialing the front desk. She didn't want to say something in the heat of the moment she would later regret.

When the night clerk answered, she calmly expressed her concerns about room 502 and its open door.

Clearing his throat, the clerk explained.

Kat listened. Shaking her head and turning her back on Nicole and Mariah, she said, "Um… I see… thanks." Replacing the receiver, she turned around. Clutching the nightstand for support, she announced, "No one is staying in Room 502."

## Chapter 31

**The** silence in room 419 was welcomed as the three prepared to turn in for the night. Mariah, on the rollaway, turned to her side and watched Nicole adjust the towel covering Theodora's picture then jump into bed and pull the covers around her neck.

Kat checked the entrance door, turned off the sitting room lights, and then wandered to the window to gaze at the moon and stars. *Was nighttime the guardian of the daylight… or the gateway to the other side? Maybe it was both,* she thought, climbing into bed beside her sister, then placing her black-rimmed glasses on the bedside stand. Reaching to switch off the lamp, she noticed Mariah's stare. "What?"

"Just wondering when you were going to share."

"Share what?"

Mariah didn't have to answer; her eyes said it all.

"All right," Kat hissed between clenched teeth. "The open door is a common occurrence reported by guests. It's the entrance for a set of private stairs to the penthouse on the fifth floor. Maintenance has checked and double-checked the door handle and hinges multiple times over the years and never found anything wrong."

"What about the pacing and laughter we heard?" Nicole asked.

"The desk clerk said the hotel has no explanation for the phenomena, except… the room was added to the hotel by Norman Baker. He used it for an office."

"And the clawing sounds?" Mariah asked.

"Another experience frequently reported by guests staying in this room. Explanation is that Baker had two Dobermans he kept in the penthouse as guard dogs."

"So, the door and sounds from 502 are all connected to Norman Baker?"

"Yep," Kat answered as she clicked the light off.

The three lay in the dark, lost in their own thoughts. Nicole found the darkness a sanctuary, a place to recharge and forget the things that had happened during the day: zombie takeover of Eureka Springs, vampire bar fight, and ghost hunter madness on every floor of the hotel.

Kat welcomed the darkness. She needed that sense of stepping out of the craziness for a while. With time, she knew she could find a scientific explanation for everything that had happened.

Mariah dreaded the darkness, the domain of the dead. Certain more was to come; she waited for the next move in the ghostly game of cat-and-mouse.

Minute by minute, the hotel grew quieter as the clock ticked closer to midnight. The darkness and the sweet lullaby of silence finally lulled the guests into a dreamless sleep.

# Chapter 32

**The** pitter-patter of paws awakened Mariah. With the fluffy flop of Morris on the bed, she sat up and wiped the sleep from her eyes. Obviously, all the work Nicole had done salting the room was wasted on her ghostly friend.

Mariah briefly massaged her temples as she glanced at the bedside clock. A few minutes after midnight. Seeing Kat stir, she laid back down and pulled Morris close, pretending to be asleep.

Kat's eyes snapped open. She was not sure what had awakened her. *Was it a presence lingering nearby, watching and listening?* She shivered, paranoid that the horror from the morgue may have followed them to the room.

Kat tried to fully awaken while checking on her roommates. Nicole was snuggled down in the covers beside her, and Mariah was curled up on the rollaway. She next made a quick sweep around the room, looking for anything out of place. She warily eyed the mahogany wardrobe in one corner. *Just the kind of place something or someone would hide,* she thought before moving on.

Finding nothing suspicious, she stumbled to the bathroom. Relieved to find only one reflection in the mirror, she filled a glass with water, tucked a few wayward hairs behind her ear, then had a long drink. Returning to bed, her inner self scolded, *Rational explanations, not ghosts. Don't let your imagination run wild.* Closing her eyes, Kat willed her body and mind to relax. Before long, the hum of the air-conditioner lured her back to sleep.

Mariah was glad Morris was content to lie wrapped in her arms until Kat passed out. The twitching of his tail signaled her feline friend had had enough snuggling and was plotting an escape.

Wiggling free, Morris sat inches away from Mariah's face and blinked several times. Turning away, he jumped from the bed, ran into the sitting room, and sat in front of the entrance door. When Mariah didn't follow, Morris returned to the bedroom door and sat upright. Vigilant, ears pointed up and forward, he waited for his friend to roll out of bed. Instead, she rolled over and faced the wall, hoping he would give up and go away.

These midnight adventures with the ghost cat were becoming a habit she did not want to encourage. After a few minutes, she peeked over her shoulder to see if the pesky fur ball had moved on.

Nope. There he sat, alert and watchful, tail slowly swishing.

"Okay," she whispered, giving in. Shoving feet into fuzzy slippers, Mariah tip-toed from the room. Good thing she was an expert escape artist. Her attempts to sneak out of her parents' house as a teen were the stuff of legends. Mariah considered it a harmless prank and had enjoyed the thrill of escaping and hanging out with friends when she was supposed to have been home in bed. She had very fond memories of creeping out the door or shimmying down the trellis well past curfew.

Mariah's parents, on the other hand, had taken the teenage antics more seriously. They'd tried everything from securing the windows to hanging bells on the doors to protect their wayward daughter from what they considered dangerous situations, un-healthy temptations, and dicey choices.

The door creaked as it opened, and Morris made his escape. Mariah was more cautious. She stood motionless for a second, then peeked into the hall. Dead silence. Nothing moved. Looking over her shoulder to make sure Kat and Nicole were still asleep, she stepped over the threshold, then closed the door behind.

The carpeted hallway muffled the sound of her footsteps as she rounded the corner of the fourth floor. Stopping at the elevator where Morris was waiting, she was struck by the utter absence of sound. *Quiet as a graveyard,* she thought.

Pushing the red arrow for the elevator, the two waited together until the doors slid open. Once inside, Mariah scanned the control panel and chose a floor.

She heard music before the doors opened.

The sound grew louder as she followed Morris from the elevator to the empty lobby. At first, the sound mimicked organ music she remembered hearing when she had attended Sunday services with her grandmother. When asked why an organ instead of the piano, she

177

remembered her grandmother saying, "The organ has always been considered, and rightly so, the king of musical instruments; it's comforting because it has the ability to make all the sounds of creation." But hearing it now, in this hotel, Mariah did not find the organ music reassuring.

The music gradually took on a dark tone and grew to sound more like an evil, deranged, psychotic lunatic with some unholy musical ability was sitting at the keyboard. The ghastly and macabre music, straight from some horror film, filled Mariah with dread.

The playing became more intense and frantic as she walked slowly along the hall to the sitting area where the sound was coming from. An antique pipe organ sat on one side of the lobby like a giant wooden box of whistles.

The music abruptly stopped.

Hoping to find some sort of musical entertainment for late-night guests taking place, she really wasn't surprised to find the lobby deserted: no guests, desk clerk, doorman, or organist. *Was this one of Dr. Baker's organs? Is this why Morris dragged me on this ghost hunt?*

Moving closer to the roped-off organ, she skimmed the exhibit, hoping to find the answer. She discovered the organ had been constructed around early 1912 and was one of three models still known to exist. The other two were in museums in Germany and Japan.

*Interesting information, but if this isn't one of Baker's organs, why did Morris lead me here?* she wondered.

Turning, she searched the lobby for her furry friend. She finally spotted him curled up on the sofa next to a silver-haired man wearing a white suit and purple tie. Sitting straight and rigid, his cold eyes stared at the flames dancing in the white, stone fireplace.

*So, the soul of Norman Baker is bound in limbo between life and death. Why does his spirit linger? What is it hoping to find peace? Forgiveness?* Mariah wondered on her way back to room 419.

## Chapter 33

**The** three women sat next to each other at one of the tables in the Crystal Ballroom, surrounded by other diners hoping to communicate with the spirits residing in the hotel. The huge windows, hardwood floors, and shimmering crystal chandeliers descending from the high ceiling offered the perfect backdrop for the dinner theater.

The waitstaff finished clearing tables as the lights dimmed. The audience fell silent, and all eyes turned to the stage along the back wall. The black curtains parted, and the master of ceremonies stepped forward. "Welcome to an unforgettable evening of magic and mystery. On the heels of last year's astonishing and hair-raising Halloween séance—Intrigue heater stars, illusionist Sean-Paul and ghost-talker Juliana Fay, return to the Crescent Hotel in an attempt to connect with the spirits that visit the rooms and roam the hallways of America's most haunted hotel."

Mariah listened to the voice coming from the stage, but her attention was hijacked by an uneasy feeling creeping into her mind. It began as soft murmurs from the shadows. She tried to shrug it off, but when the whispers became more persistent, she couldn't ignore the "calling" any longer and allowed her eyes to roam. Skipping over tables of excited spectators, she probed the four corners of the room.

In the darkness, she found the "Gathering," spirits of guests who had checked out… but never left, huddling in the darkness, waiting and watching.

*"I see you. I hear you,"* Mariah silently whispered. Willing her mind to sever the connection, she switched back to the man with the microphone.

"The first part of the show will feature Sean-Paul conducting a demonstration of hypnosis inspired by the great turn of the century mentalist Howard Thurston, a stage magician. In the second half of the show, Julianna Fay, channeling the spirit of Annie Fay, an early medium around the time of Houdini, will conduct a séance.

"The couple's Vaudeville-era performance is guaranteed to leave you on the edge of your seat from start to finish. So, sit back and enjoy the show," the announcer invited as the curtains swept aside, revealing the husband-and-wife duo.

Over the applause, Kat pointed out, "If this is half as entertaining as the couple's performance we experienced on our last Eureka Springs adventure, be prepared to be amused and amazed."

The two entertainers took center stage in lavish costumes inspired by the Victorian "Golden Age" of magic. In a red-and-gold, single-breasted vest and knee-length black form-fitting jacket, Sean-Paul twirled Juliana across the stage. The black ruffles of the ghost-talker's burlesque, showgirl costume swirled around her thighs, highlighting the striking figure of the fair-complected performer.

"You do realize we have broken every taboo activity on our parents' list with this impromptu girls-get-away, right? Magic… hypnosis… a séance…"

Kat interrupted her sister. "We haven't completely crossed over to the dark side; no one has gotten a tattoo."

"There's still time," Mariah chuckled, winking at Kat as the handsome, blond-haired, blue-eyed illusionist relieved the announcer of his microphone.

"The Crescent Hotel is ground zero for Halloween fun. Proclaimed America's most haunted hotel by investigators of one of the most popular paranormal TV shows, visitors from all over the United States travel to this resort hoping for an extraordinary experience with one of the hotel guests from the past," Sean-Paul explained as he left the stage to walk among the tables, interacting with members of the audience.

After a few minutes of greeting guests and asking where they were from, the illusionist picked up where he had left off. "The hotel gained its reputation in part thanks to a man named Norman Baker; a former vaudeville magician and hypnotist who bought the hotel in the late nineteen-thirties. As a tribute to Baker, I will bring audience members to the stage and put them under a sleep-like trance." The master mentalist finished with, "Any volunteers?"

Hands went up all over the room. On his way back to the stage, Sean-Paul chose members from the audience to join him.

When he passed their table, Nicole grabbed Kat's hand before she could volunteer. "No! You have no filter, no control. I can only imagine what you would do or say when freed from all social constraints and put in a trance."

Kat jerked free and put her hand down. "Oh, for heaven's sake. Hypnotized people may seem to lose control of themselves, but, in reality, they're just very relaxed and open to suggestion."

Once on stage, Juliana Fay invited the participants to take a seat. While getting comfortable, Sean-Paul thanked the four for agreeing to be hypnotized and explained, "You will simply be in a deeply relaxed state. You will be completely aware of what you are doing, and I will not be able to make you do anything you don't want to do."

Taking a vintage gold watch from his front vest pocket, the hypnotist held it up in front of the volunteers. Running his free hand down the chain to steady the timepiece until it was still, he then set it in a back-and-forth motion.

Speaking slowly, in a soothing voice, he said, "Follow the watch with your eyes and listen to the sound of my voice. Don't look around at me or anyone else. Keep your eyes on my watch. Do not blink. Do not look away."

As the participants and audience concentrated on the object at the end of the chain, Sean-Paul gave the next instructions. "Breathe in through your nose and out through your mouth… nice and easy, focusing on your breathing Let go of all your tension and stress, allowing your mind to rest."

Planting the first suggestion, he said, "You feel your whole body getting heavy, your arms, your legs, and, especially, your head. Now, take a deep breath, relax your neck, and let your head tilt forward gently and slowly, all the way to your chest… and sleep. From this point on, your eyes will stay firmly shut until I tell you to open them."

Heads bowed and shoulders relaxed, the volunteers appeared to fall asleep sitting in their chairs. One woman slumped to the right, resting her head on the shoulder of the man next to her, and a young man, limp as a rag doll, slid slowly from his chair to the floor.

After the laughter died down, Sean-Paul said, "Now, on the count of three, open your eyes and sit up in your chair. One… two…

three." Following instructions, the man on the floor took his seat while the other three sat up and looked out at the audience, eyes blank.

Starting with the first chair, the mentalist asked, "What is your name?" The man adjusted the collar of his business suit and answered, "John D. Howell, Jr."

"John, when I snap my fingers, you will forget your name." With a single snap, Sean Paul asked, "What is your name?"

"My name is…" John paused and shook his head as if trying to clear his mind, then tried again, "My name is…" Bewildered, John looked at Sean-Paul and admitted sadly, "I don't remember my name." This revelation brought a chuckle from his family sitting at one of the tables near the stage.

Sean-Paul stepped in front of the hypnotized man and said, "When I snap my fingers, you will remember your name." As a loud snap echoed across the room, the question was repeated.

Without hesitating, grinning from ear to ear, the man answered, "John D. Howell, Jr."

After the clapping faded, the performance moved on to the next guest. "What is your name and where are you from?"

With a very distinct southern drawl, the young woman answered, "My name is Charlotte, and I am from Atlanta, Georgia."

"Charlotte from Atlanta, Georgia, hold up both hands. How many fingers do you have?"

Without looking at her hands, the young lady from Georgia answered, "Ten."

"Count them," Sean-Paul instructed, pointing to each finger as the young woman counted from one to ten. "Now, when I snap my fingers, you will forget the number six."

Sean-Paul snapped and said, "Count your fingers as I point to them."

Charlotte looked at her hand and started counting. "One, two, three, four, five…" and stopped. Realizing something was not right, she looked intently at her hand and began recounting, stopping again after five. As if mentally calculating a challenging math problem, she scrutinized each finger, one at a time. Her face lit up. "Oh, I got this!" she declared with a touch of pride.

Starting over, Charlotte counted each finger as it was pointed to. At finger number six, she proudly called out, "Seven!" and continued counting. After reaching ten, she stopped, realizing there was one last finger to count. Not understanding, she looked back over her outstretched hands. Stumped for a minute, she stared into space, then delighted with her solution, Charlotte looked up at Sean-Paul. "Eleven," she announced, bringing a gust of laughter from the floor.

Sean-Paul congratulated the young woman on her excellent counting skills and then issued one last instruction. "When I snap my fingers, you will remember the number six."

After the snap, Charlotte completed a flawless count, which was immediately rewarded with a round of blusterous applause.

Once the guest from Georgia was seated, the show moved on to the third chair, the rag doll who had slid to the stage floor. After a few questions, the audience discovered the young man's name was Kevin, a student at the University of Arkansas.

With a mischievous smile, the hypnotist gave Kevin a set of instructions to follow. "When I snap my fingers, you will hop three times like a bunny rabbit and then sit back in your chair." With the snap of fingers and chanting of "Kevin, Kevin, Kevin" from his college buddies, the young man stood, twitched his nose side to side, wagged an imaginary tail, and hopped three times with his hands held in front before returning to his seat. Members of the audience all across the dining room held up cell phones in an effort to video the performance.

Mariah pointed out, "I bet one of Kevin's fraternity brothers posts that online tonight, and, by tomorrow, the video goes viral."

Kat couldn't stifle the giggles that escaped when she said, "And Kevin will be an internet star."

Nicole turned to her sister. "What are you laughing about? That could've been you doing the bunny hop across the stage. I saved you from the biggest scandal to ever hit southwest Missouri."

Used to her sister's harassment, Kat defended herself. "I think Missouri has survived bigger controversies," she said, turning back to the stage in time to catch the hypnotist introducing the last volunteer.

"Let's hear it for, Renee Sullivan, the last contestant in tonight's Crescent Hotel's Halloween dance contest." The audience clapped wildly, anticipating what was to come.

Turning to Renee, Sean-Paul said, "When I snap my fingers, you will perform your best 60s' dance routine, then sit back in your chair." With the snap of fingers, the woman, easily in her seventies, launched into a wild version of The Twist. Hips swiveling, arms swinging backward and forward as if she was drying her backside with a towel, Renee took to the stage and danced to music only she could hear.

The impromptu dance routine brought down the house. People clapped, whistled, and stomped their feet in encouragement. Out of breath, the dance contestant bowed and then collapsed in her chair.

Crossing in front of the four waiting for further instructions, the master hypnotist requested of the audience, "Let's give our friends a round of applause for their cooperation and entertainment."

After the noise and laughter subsided, he turned to the volunteers and said, "Now, I'm going to count backward from five, and when I reach one, you're going to be released from hypnosis. You'll be awake, back to normal, and remember everything that took place on the stage."

On the count of one, the volunteers gave themselves a mental shake while, at the same time, sat up a little straighter in their chairs. John shook his head, not understanding how he could have forgotten his name. Charlotte looked at her hands in confusion. The bunny-hopper laughed out loud, remembering his rabbit impersonation. But the Dancing Queen stole the hearts of the audience, with a flirtatious wink and a Miss-America- wave to her new fans. Cheered erupted as the two women and two men were escorted from the stage, making way for part two of the Halloween dinner theater.

## Chapter 34

**The** dark room was like a place out of time—a time in history, decades ago, when it had been a popular pastime for people to gather in parlors and sitting rooms to perform the rituals of the *séance.*

Nicole leaned across the table and addressed her sister, "So, reading over the long list of resort activities, you decided communicating with the spirits of the dead was the best choice for tonight?"

"Yeah, what happened to s'mores around the firepit or the bluegrass concert in the park?" Mariah asked.

Nicole shrugged, not happy, but realizing the alternative could have been much worse, acknowledged, "I guess we can be thankful you didn't grab a Ouija board and drag us off to the Eureka Springs Cemetery."

"Have to admit, I was tempted, but I've seen enough horror movies to know better," Kat replied, not fazed by the criticism.

The ghost-talker, Julianna Fay, lit three candles positioned in the center of the stage table. The light formed an arc of brilliant gold in the blackness, spotlighting each of the three other faces in the circle. By the flickering yellow, the shapes of the furniture and people seated around the Crystal Ballroom were discernible, but the colors so muted that they were almost gray.

Soon, the flames melted the white wax. A puddle of hot liquid gathered around each wick and spilled over the sides, dripping onto the black table covering. Slowly, the aromatic smell of sandalwood permeated the ballroom.

Mariah took a long deep breath—the fresh fragrance immediately filled her lungs and calmed her chaotic thoughts. In the darkness that stole even her own form, she was content to sit back and let the events about to unfold on stage take their course. In a couple of days, they would be heading home. Hopefully, stepping out of the craziness, with their ghost wars behind them, her two friends would move on to a more manageable obsession.

Looking out into the darkness, Julianna Fay addressed the audience. "Everyone, close your eyes and breathe with me… slowly and deeply, in through your nose and out through your mouth. As you exhale, allow yourself to feel the calming effect of leaving all worries and concerns behind. Continue to breathe, and, as you do, I want you to imagine the candlelight glowing across your shoulders and onto the shoulders of the person on either side… connecting our energy… connecting us all to the candlelight. As the glow encircles the room, its power of protection spreads, and its power to gather the spirits strengthens."

Giving the audience a few moments to rest in the protection of the light, she continued, "Once the séance begins, you may experience things. You may notice a temperature change, or a touch, or you might sense someone standing next to you or behind you. Do not be afraid. Remember, you are protected by the light." To the two women and one man seated at the table, she said, "Take the hand of the person on either side of you and try to relax."

Placing three black-and-white pictures, one in front of each volunteer, she instructed, "Think of a few things you would like to ask the person in the photograph before we get started. It's best to use yes-or-no questions because we will get clearer answers."

Before beginning the séance, the ghost-talker provided the audience with a brief overview of the hotel's history. "The majestic Crescent Hotel was built by the Eureka Springs Improvement Company and the Frisco Railroad. Featuring electric bells, steam heat, and a hydraulic elevator, the hotel was completed in 1886 at a cost of just over a quarter of a million dollars.

"At the time, it was considered the most fabulous and fascinating resort west of the Mississippi. Today, the 1886 Crescent Hotel is known not only for its historic Victorian beauty, but also for its active array of spirits. Tonight, we hope to connect with several of the more notorious guests from the past." Touching each candle, she said, "We invite the spirits of the hotel to the light and warmth."

From the four corners, Mariah spied white silhouettes waltzing from the shadows. They moved to a melody of misery and pain from an invisible orchestra of supernatural musicians as they danced their way to the light.

As the lost souls gathered on the stage, the symphony of whispered sorrow rose and then fell silent.

Mariah finally got up the courage to steal a glance at her friends and found them patiently waiting along with everyone else in the room for something to happen on stage. Mariah realized she was the only witness to the ghostly ball and raised her eyes heavenward. *Why me?* she silently whispered. *I never asked to inherit this superpower.* Then a tiny voice in her head suggested, *maybe you will eventually find a way to put it to good use.*

Giving herself a mental shake, she returned to reality and the séance. Julianna welcomed the spirits of the Crescent Hotel and then requested, "Spirits, please make your presence known. Give us a sign."

Mariah felt the energy in the room intensify just before the rapping began. It started on the outer walls, causing guests to yelp with fright and twist in their chairs, following the progression of knocks to the stage. The loud banging caused the séance table to wobble and the candles to sputter, but the circle of hands held.

The ghost-talker began connecting with the spirit world by concentrating on each of the people in the photographs. Touching the first picture, she spoke to the audience,

"Michael was one of the Irish masons who helped build the hotel in 1884. While working on the roof, it's said he lost his balance while flirting with a passing young woman and fell to his death. Now, he makes his presence known from in Room 218."

Juliana focused on the picture for a few seconds before continuing. "Michael, if you are with us, rap twice for, yes."

The spirit answered with two knocks, getting gasps from the audience.

Looking at the first volunteer, a woman in her early twenties, Julianna asked, "What is your question for Michael?"

"Do you like women?"

The loud and boisterous rapping by the spirit brought a burst of laughter from the audience, who apparently found it funny that Michal's untimely demise had not affected the Irishman's fancy for young women.

Once the noise died down, the volunteer continued with her questioning, "What's it like to live in the spirit world?" Not an inquiry that could be answered with a simple yes or no, the members of the audience held their breath, hoping for a reply.

When Michael did not respond, Julianna repeated the question, and the room fell into an eerie silence. As the suspense built, the ghost-talker raised a hand to one ear, signaling she was listening to a voice only she could hear. "I'm getting a message."

All movement ceased and all eyes focused on the face showcased in the flickering candlelight.

Looking off into the distance, Julianna channeled Michael's response, "Lonely." The one-word answer startled some in the audience, and a sad moan escaped and rose from several tables.

Brushing fingers along the edges of the next photograph, Juliana summarized Baker's story, "In 1937, a man named Norman Baker bought the Crescent Hotel and turned it into the Baker Cancer Hospital. Claiming to have the cure for many ailments, he used various unorthodox methods of treatment. His most sought-after remedy, Formula #5, touted as a miracle cure for cancer, turned out to be a deadly concoction that killed not cured.

Juliana paused to let the guests digest the information. Sensing she, once again, had everyone's attention, she summoned the spirit, then asked, "Norman Baker, are you with us?" Getting only silence, Juliana insisted, more forcefully, "Norman Baker, are you with us?"

Mariah could sense the spirit's reluctance to communicate with the living. In death, as in life, Baker resented being questioned about any part of his past. She could feel the spirit's anger growing as a cold chill crawled across the room.

Guests shivered, pulling jackets and sweaters close. Nicole, along with several others, grabbed for one of the temperature gauges randomly placed on tables during the intermission by Sean-Paul. "You are not going to believe this," she said, passing the thermometer to Mariah. "The temperature has dropped almost twenty degrees from the time I checked it at the beginning of the séance."

"Someone probably cranked up the AC for dramatic effect," Kat said.

"Oh, please, don't be such a cynic," Nicole insisted. "It's him. It's Baker. He wants everyone to know he's here, and, from the chill in the air, he's not happy about his command performance."

Unable to resist the calling of the light, the spirit finally answered with two hard raps.

Juliana nodded at the second volunteer,

a well-dressed older man, indicating it was his turn.

"I have three questions. First, were you really a doctor?" The spirit was quick to answer with two knocks which caused an outbreak of whispered comments from the people seated near the stage.

"Was your Formula #5 a cure for cancer?" Again, two hard knocks could be heard.

A faint rumbling of displeasure rolled across the room, indicating the audience did not believe the spirit.

"Did any of your patients die from cancer?" The answer was not forthcoming, and the crowd waited.

The spirit of Norman Baker seemed unwilling to answer, choosing to put on a show first. The candle flames began to dance, popping and cracking, spitting hot melted wax. Finally, with one last loud pop, the spirit answered with a single bang on the table.

Someone from the audience yelled, "Liar!" causing a flurry of disparaging remarks from other guests who agreed with the characterization.

Kat, known to tell a "little" white lie from time to time, couldn't keep quiet, "Hmmmm, who would have thought it? Ghosts aren't to be trusted."

"If the living struggle with telling the truth, the whole truth, and nothing but the truth, I guess it only makes sense that the dead would struggle with it, too," Mariah pointed out. Refusing to be drawn into a debate over the merits of telling the truth with a known storyteller, she turned her attention back to the séance.

Pointing to the last photograph, Juliana explained that the spirit of Theodora was known to visit suite 419. It was believed she was either a nurse or patient at the infamous Eureka Springs cancer hospital. Concentrating on the photograph, she asked if Theodora was present and, after getting an answer, Juliana nodded to the last volunteer, a woman with thinning white hair, for the next question.

"Were you a patient or were you a nurse at the Baker Cancer Hospital?" Although the question asked by the woman could not be answered with a simple yes or no, it was clear that everyone seated in the room remained hopeful as all eyes turned to Julianna.

Soon the ghost-talker became involved

in a whispered back-and-forth conversation with the spirit world. Eyes closed, head tilted to one side, she appeared to strain to catch each word. At last, she nodded and spoke directly to the spirit. "Yes," Julianna answered, confirming she understood the silent query.

Anticipation moved quickly through the quiet room. The only sound was the ragged breathing and beating of human hearts. The silence was broken when Julianna opened her eyes and slowly stared at the fluttering candle.

At that moment, the spirit of Theodora spoke directly through the ghost-talker. The cryptic message, with its hidden meaning, was the perfect mysterious ending to an evening no one would soon forget.

*"Shrouded in the skin of a healer,*
*a man more vile than the devil,*
*once ruled a place more foul than Hades."*

# Chapter 35

**Creative** *minds are rarely tidy,* Kat reasoned. As her anxiety grew, so did the mess, her focus so scattered that it was a challenge to get everything in good order before her two roommates returned. When the key turned in the lock and the door swung open, Kat realized she had left the cleanup too late.

The first thing Nicole and Mariah noticed upon entering the suite after their yoga workout was the takeout container of salsa and chips abandoned on the coffee table. Dropping gym bags by the door, they followed the crumbs to the bedroom.

Stepping over piles of paper and clutter of books scattered across the floor, they just stood and stared. In the corner, the trash overflowed with a wad of plastic bags. A cup of coffee sat on the nightstand, untouched. Around it, strips of cut paper spilled over the edge to the floor and poked out from under the bed.

"Where in the hell did you get all this?" Nicole demanded, pointing to the pictures ripped from open books, scissors, markers, tacks, and colored yarn coating the bed in thick piles.

"My new friend, Benny," Kat answered while pushing glasses up on her nose and frantically trying to smooth the wild mess of red hair back into place.

"Benny?"

"Our shuttle driver from the Voodoo Lounge. He knows all the art supply stores in the area. We took a quick detour to the Eureka Springs Historical Museum, where the curator helped me locate a few copies of old newspaper articles related to the hotel. The books, I picked up in the lobby. They have dozens of paperbacks, with pictures, about the history of the Crescent Hotel.

Waving her hand across the room, Nicole confronted her sister. "Well, this might make sense if you were an artist."

Mariah teased, "Yeah, so far, all your masterpieces have been pencil sketches of stick figures which I'm sure most art critics would find lacking in depth and imagination."

"Giving in to your creative urges, you splurged on art supplies. Fine, but did you have to trash the entire suite in pursuit of artistic fulfillment?" Nicole scolded.

Mariah gave the room *a* quick once-over before adding, "I didn't think it was possible, but this is worse than your teacher desk at the high school."

"In my defense," Kat said, "a messy desk is a sign of genius, according to science. Thomas Edison, Albert Einstein, and Steve Jobs all had messy desks."

Hands-on hips, Nicole informed her sister, "One, there are always exceptions to every rule. Two, where we sleep is *not* a substitute for your desk."

Mariah finished for Nicole with a crooked smile, "And, three, you are *no* genius."

Used to being hit by wave after wave of criticism from both her sister and friend, Kat only shook her head. "Oh, ye of little faith," she admonished, pointing to the white Styrofoam board propped up on the dresser.

"What's this?" Nicole asked, stepping closer to look at the collage of pictures, post-it notes, and newspaper articles pinned to the white board and interconnected with colored yarn. The words, "Case of America's Most Haunted Hotel," printed in all caps with a black marker at the top of the board, grabbed her attention first. She rolled her eyes heavenward. "Jack, or in this case, *Jane* of all trades, master of none: kidnapper, travel agent, and ghost hunter."

"A woman of many talents. I'm proud to call her friend," Mariah pronounced with a smirk.

"Just hear me out. After the séance last night, I realized we've been approaching this paranormal mystery thing all wrong. Instead of investigating and trying to prove ghosts exist, we should be thinking like detectives: searching for clues, collecting evidence, interviewing witnesses, and following the facts."

Mariah pointed to the obvious, "Might be a little difficult interviewing witnesses… they're all *dead*."

"This should make perfect sense to you," Kat said, looking at Nicole. "You read every Nancy Drew Mystery before your twelfth birthday and just recently binge-watched seasons one through ten of the *CSI* and *Law and Order* series."

"Flickering lights, fleeting shadows, and the occasional bump in the night… who do you call, a paranormal investigator or a ghost detective?" Nicole mocked.

"There's a difference?" Mariah challenged.

Kat cocked her head to one side and thought for a moment before answering. "First, I think it's important to note that, despite the fact that many people believe in ghosts, science overwhelmingly denies their existence; there has never been any evidence put forth confirming ghosts are real or that a particular location is inhabited by spirits of the dead."

Losing patience, Nicole asked, "So?"

"Just hear me out," Kat reasoned. "Ghost hunters and ghost detectives are alike, in that they investigate unexplained occurrences, including anything from strange noises and slamming doors to floating objects and apparitions. The difference is in their core beliefs. The ghost hunters' philosophy involves accepting things that defy the known laws of nature and have not been verified by scientists. These phantom sleuths attempt to collect evidence supporting the existence of paranormal activity. On the other hand, detectives are problem-solvers, employing scientific methods and critical thinking to get to the bottom of suspected hauntings. They attempt to collect evidence to confirm the activity has a scientific explanation."

"Sounds like your usual word salad," Mariah announced, questioning Kat's debate technique of confusing the opponent.

"You *are* aware of the fact that some very famous and totally believable people have reported experiencing paranormal activity?" Nicole questioned.

"Name one," Kat dared.

"Okay. Shortly after World War II ended, Prime Minister Winston Churchill visited President Franklin Roosevelt at the White House. He stayed in the room Lincoln used as a bedroom during his term in office.

Churchill reported that one night, after a long bath with a Scotch and cigar, he walked naked into the adjoining bedroom, where he was met by the ghost of Abraham Lincoln. Churchill claimed the president flashed him a smile then vanished."

Kat was not convinced and attempted to debunk the prime minister's claim. "It doesn't take a scientist to explain Churchill's run-in with Lincoln. It was common knowledge that the ghost of President Lincoln sometimes surprised guests with his presence. So, the sighting was probably a combination of factors: exhaustion from managing a four-year war, the suggestion that the White

House was haunted, and let's not forget the Scotch."

"Churchill in the tub, whisky in one hand and a cigar in the other is a picture that will stick with me for a long time." Mariah chuckled.

Eyebrows raised, Nicole considered her options and then looked from Mariah to her sister. Brushing a pile of trash from the bed, she sat and offered Mariah a seat. "Let's give the rookie detective a chance to make a fool of herself."

"Okay, Sherlock, give it your best shot," Mariah challenged.

# Chapter 36

**Kat** loved a challenge and was eager to make her case. Putting on her best game face, she got down to business. "There are decades of reported activities at the Crescent Hotel attributed to the paranormal. These rumors have inspired many investigations. Ghost-hunting teams from all over the United States have probed every nook and cranny of the hotel, using electronic devices like night vision cameras and EMF meters. Noises and images captured with the technology only prove that there are sights and sounds in the halls and rooms that our senses cannot detect. In my opinion, it doesn't prove the existence of rogue spirits running amuck at the hotel."

Mariah interrupted with a challenge, "After our morgue tour, I don't think you can keep denying something isn't going on here."

Passionate about following the truth, Kat

responded, "I agree something is definitely off the rails here, but let's look at it through the lens of science and see if there's a plausible explanation that can be verified with facts."

Mariah glanced at Nicole to see if she was on board with this idea, then agreed. "Okay, we're listening."

Getting the go-ahead, the ghost detective proceeded to present her evidence to her team. Picking up a pencil, she pointed to the center of the Styrofoam board from which all lines of yarn originated. Beside the photo of the Crescent Hotel was a map of Arkansas with the town of Eureka Springs circled, and, for an added touch, the highway from Branson, Missouri, to the hotel was highlighted in red marker.

Nicole clapped her hands like an excited child and whispered to Mariah, "Isn't this cool? I've always loved it when detectives in movies are cracking down on a case, and they go to their evidence board where they've connected the clues with string, and all they need is that final piece."

"You're watching too much TV," Mariah whispered back.

Unaware of the back-and-forth between her teammates, Kat continued making her case. "The Crescent Hotel is at the center of our investigation. I've only posted physical evidence because detectives consider it the most reliable. That's the reason for the pictures and profiles of real people and events documented to be directly connected to the hotel. I've included eyewitness testimony only when it's important to understanding one of these profiles."

Both Nicole and Mariah nodded. Nicole responded, "That makes sense."

Noting that there were no dissenters, Kat began presenting her evidence. "Built in 1886 by the Eureka Improvement Company, the hotel opened on May 20, 1886, with a banquet and ball for over four hundred people. Since then, there have been hundreds of tales of paranormal experiences at the hotel. Given its history, it's not surprising."

Tracing the red yarn to the picture of a young man, she explained," An Irishman named Michael was the first recorded death. He is reported to haunt room 218. Guests staying in 218 tell stories of lights turning off and on, windows opening, doors closing, and footsteps being heard in the room."

Continuing her history lesson, Kat pointed to the next picture on the evidence board. "Dr. C.F. Ellis practiced homeopathic medicine for over forty years. There was no better place to practice this type of medicine than Eureka Springs, where the cures for kidney disease, cancer, and even blindness were attributed to the local spring water. Dr. Ellis lived at 44 Prospect Avenue, next door to the hotel, and, from 1886 to 1902, he was the house physician for the resort.

Many guests and members of the hotel staff have reported that, on the second floor, a man believed to be Dr. Ellis is often seen exiting the elevator and walking across the hall to room 212, which is believed was his office. Eyewitness accounts claim that if the door happens to be closed, he just walks through it. The aroma of pipe tobacco is reported to often accompany the doctor's appearance."

Kat paused and eyed her fellow detectives. "Here is where Dr. Ellis's story takes an interesting detour. He didn't die at the hotel. Ellis owned a building on Spring Street in the historic downtown area. The structure was destroyed by fire in March of 1931. Ellis died of heart failure as he watched his building destroyed."

Nicole's eyebrows shot up. Absently brushing aside bangs that obscured her vision, she asked, "What? He didn't die at the hotel? How is this possible if his spirit haunts the second floor?"

"I know; baffling, isn't it? But wait, the hotel's story gets even more intriguing." She glanced at her notes. "The next few years, there were no reported deaths at the Crescent. The resort was sold to C.H. Smith of St. Louis in 1901. In 1902, the Frisco Railroad leased the property from Smith for five years. But the resort's luck didn't last long. From 1908 to 1923 and again from 1929-1933, the building became the Crescent College and Conservatory for young women, functioning as a hotel during the summer months. One suspected death is that of a student from the college who either jumped or fell from the third-floor balcony. Although there is no record of this event over the years, people report seeing a girl in the mist fall from the balcony."

Nicole interrupted, pointing to the next picture labeled, Breckie. "On my way to the room the other night, I ran into some girls on the second floor playing with a ball outside their room. They told me they were trying to get that boy to join them."

Kat explained, "Unfortunately, several children have passed away at the hotel, and the boy is one of them. In 1910, Richard Thompson became president of the Crescent College. His son, Breckie, died in 1918 of an intestinal infection, and it's reported the young boy is seen throughout the hotel, often bouncing a ball."

Kat tapped the picture of Norman Baker. "The Crescent Hotel closed in 1937, and, after some renovations, the Baker Cancer Hospital opened its doors. Here is where our friend Theodora comes into the story. There's record of her being at the hotel during this time, but it's unclear what she was doing here at the clinic."

"We have firsthand experience with the shenanigans of Theodora. I'm more interested in what you uncovered about Baker while playing private detective," Mariah declared, toying with the thick braid of hair dangling over her shoulder.

Enjoying the limelight and calling on all her college acting skills, Kat delivered the cliffhanger as dramatically as if she were a character in a television show. "Time was running out for Baker. He should have heeded the Missouri slogan used to remind people of the dangers of traveling a road where it's too hard to tell how deep the water is: turn around, don't drown."

## Chapter 37

**Pulling** a flask from her back jeans pocket, Kat unscrewed the lid and took a big swig. "Time for a break," she announced, passing the container to her sister.

"What's this?" Nicole asked cautiously, taking a sip before passing the leather-bound, metal container to Mariah.

"Salted caramel moonshine," Kat answered, licking a drop from her lower lip.

Mariah took a long drink, wiped her mouth with the back of one hand, then passed the flask back to Kat. "And where in the hell did you get moonshine?"

Kat didn't answer, but just smiled an irritating smart-aleck smile that both her friend and sister absolutely hated.

Mariah and Nicole both thought for a moment, then looked at each other and back at Miss Know-It-All and yelled in unison, "Benny!"

"Bingo!" Kat declared.

The three sat, passing the flask between them until, at last empty, Kat screwed the lid on and placed it on the dresser beside the evidence board.

"Now, for the ending of the Norman Baker story and on to the next chapter of the hotel," Kat announced. "The Baker Cancer Clinic was a big success. People with cancer and a whole host of other diseases flocked to the hospital, many signing away their life's savings for the fake cures, a mixture of watermelon seed, brown cornsilk, alcohol, and carbolic acid."

"I know what the first three ingredients are, but what is carbolic acid?" Mariah asked.

"Carbolic acid is a very poisonous chemical substance that can cause inflammation, vomiting, convulsions, paralysis, and even death," Kat replied after referring to her notes.

"That's horrible. How could he do such a monstrous thing to people who trusted him?" Nicole wondered aloud.

"Money. It was all about the money. I discovered Baker had accumulated hundreds of thousands of dollars from the use of his fake cures for the three years the Eureka Springs

Hospital was in operation. He kept his millions in various safe deposit boxes known only to him and his mistress, Thelma Yount."

"Why did the hospital close after such a short time if it was such a money-maker?" Nicole asked.

"There was good reason for its closure," Kat declared. "When Baker began mailing flyers touting his new Eureka Springs hospital and the benefits of his miracle treatment, the government got involved. Eventually the US post office charged Baker with using the mail to defraud people. The office argued that his postal advertisements went too far with the cancer treatment claims. The case went to trial in 1940."

"Mail fraud? That's all they could get him on?" Mariah asked, disappointed in the legal system.

"The transcript of the trial I found online lists mail fraud as the only charge," Kat explained. "The document wasn't long and most of it was legal mumbo-jumbo to me, but I found the testimony of the witnesses called by the prosecutor riveting. Several hospital staff testified that, upon being admitted to the cancer clinic, patients were required to sign undated letters declaring themselves much improved. The letters were mailed to the patients' families during their stay in an effort to conceal their actual health. Next, a long line up of husbands, wives, mothers, and fathers of Baker's former patients were called to the stand. Their stories were all the same. The failed cancer treatment hastened the death of their loved ones. As the cancers advanced and it was evident the patient would not recover, they were declared cured and sent home. However, many passed away before reaching home or shortly thereafter."

"Did Baker really think he could cure cancer or was he just simply crazy?" Nicole asked, finding it hard to believe someone could be so cold-hearted.

"A psychiatrist who evaluated him in prison believed that Baker was delusional because, despite incontrovertible evidence to the contrary, he still believed in his magic elixir cure," Kat answered.

"So, he was crazy as a Missouri bedbug," Mariah concluded.

"Well, then there's this—during the trial, the Assistant U.S. Attorney quoted Baker as saying that he would, and I quote, 'reap one million dollars out of the suckers in Arkansas.' So, I don't think we will ever know the truth behind Baker's motivation for pushing his cancer cure. Fame, fortune, or was he just a charming psychopath."

Nicole and Mariah sat in stunned silence for a few moments, trying to make sense of the cold-blooded, money-making scheme orchestrated by Baker and his associates.

"The good news—if there is any in this story—is that the court found Baker's cure a hoax and found him guilty of the charge. He was sent to four years at the United States penitentiary in Fort Leavenworth, Kansas."

Nicole noted, "Thankfully, the charlatan did suffer some consequences for his horrible deeds."

"I think the saying, 'Karma is a Bitch' may be true, at least in the Norman Baker Case," Kat said. "After Baker was released from prison, he moved to Miami, Florida. He died in 1958. He was buried in Muscatine, Iowa, in the Greenwood Cemetery." Kat paused for dramatic effect, then revealed, "The death certificate listed the cause of death as... cancer of the liver."

"Restores my faith in the universe to know there *is* justice for bad actors," Mariah stated.

Kat nodded in agreement and continued,

"The demise of Baker isn't the end of the hotel's story, though. From 1946 to 1973, four Chicago businessmen purchased the property. They offered packaged vacations, including room and bath, three meals a day, and area entertainment. Guests came from all over the United States by train to, of all places… Monett, Missouri. They were met by buses and transported to the Crescent. At the end of their week-long stay, guests hopped aboard a bus and returned to Missouri, where they finished the journey home by train."

Kat pointed her pencil at the picture of a bible. "As we learned from Ann Rhoden, a fire destroyed most of the fourth floor in 1967. This is interesting because the first recorded reports of hauntings at the hotel appeared after the fire."

Kat picked up a bottle of water from the dresser. After taking a sip, she continued, "In 1973, the hotel was sold to Crescent Heights Development of Wichita. This is when the first accounts of the hotel being haunted appear. One of the owners' wives gave an interview, which appeared in *The Enquirer* newspaper. She claimed guests had re-ported seeing ghostly figures in hallways and rooms and gliding through walls. In another newspaper interview, Robert Feagius reported seeing ghosts in the lobby and his room. And in the same article, it was reported a guest at the hotel named Anne-Marie Tayler claims to have seen a nurse pushing an old-fashioned hospital trolley in the hall outside her room, then vanish into thin air."

Jumping forward to the most recent addition to the list of resident ghosts, Kat tapped the last profile picture, a tabby cat. "In 1997, the present owners, Marty and Elise Roenigks, purchased both the Basin Park and Crescent Hotels. They embraced the Crescent's dark history and were happy to promote it as the most haunted hotel in America. During this time, a hungry kitten wandered into the resort and never left. Morris became known as the hotel's general manager for twenty-one years and was later buried on the hotel property. He is reported to be seen from time-to-time in the lobby or in the rooms of guests."

Kat tossed the pencil to the dresser and studied her audience of two. With a self-satisfied smile, she took a bow, signaling an end to the lengthy and well-documented presentation. "Any questions?"

Mariah sat back, waiting to see how Nicole would respond to the evidence summary. Much of what had been presented was just a retelling of what Mariah already knew, but she had to give Kat credit for fleshing out some previously unknown facts.

Nicole raised her hand. "Well, as much as it pains me to feed your already inflated ego, I must admit you did an outstanding job with the evidence board."

"Yes, and I also commend you on your thorough investigation, Detective," Mariah said. "But as a self-trained investigator, how did you know to look for the who, what, where, when, and why of the case?"

Finally getting the recognition she deserved for her superior investigative skills, Kat smiled. "Elementary, my Dear Watson." Not able to resist poking fun at her sister and friend, Kat held up a paperback she had picked up from the Mystery Moon Book Store in Eureka Springs and added, "As the great Sherlock Homes once said, 'It is my job to know what others do not.'"

# Chapter 38

**Leaning** to one side, Mariah rubbed her chin and pretended to study the evidence board to gain some time. Her mind raced, and her thoughts switched rapidly between ideas.

The three of them had survived the long downward spiral of the rabbit hole only to land in the frightening world of Paranormal-Land. The question was, how was she going to arrange a cease-fire in the ghost wars and get everyone back to the real world of the living without any casualties? She dug for the buckeye buried deep in her pant pocket. It gave her courage to wade in on the case.

Taking the neutral route, she looked at the lead detective. "Kat, you've definitely outdone yourself this time."

Nicole agreed but wasn't convinced her sister had proven her point. "Your cut-and-paste skills are impressive, but this does not explain why normal people from every corner of the country have reported coming face-to-face with visitors from the afterlife at the Crescent Hotel."

"I think you may be playing fast and loose with the term *normal* when referring to anyone who claims to see dead people," Kat interjected. "When it comes to inexplicable, mysterious happenings, the only logical explanation for your so-called *normal* people is often the presence of something supernatural. In the same way, *these* people are drawn to scary movies and terrifying roller coasters, believing that there are spirits of the dead looming around every corner is just plain thrilling to them."

"Well, in my experience being *normal* is vastly overrated," Nicole said.

Mariah stepped in, hoping to prevent a battle royale between the two warring factions, and addressed Kat, "You've created an intriguing reconstruction of the hotel's history, but what does all your hard work point to? Paranormal phenomena, scientific anomaly, or something totally different?"

Nicole jumped in before her sister could answer. "Based on the physical evidence and eyewitness accounts, I think the only logical conclusion is that science can be used to prove the hotel is some sort of supernatural entity."

This was a step too far for Kat. "No."

Nicole put up a hand. "Just give me a chance to present my theory."

Bad-tempered, Kat grumbled, "You've got the floor."

"In case you don't remember, I studied Einstein's Law of Conservation of Energy in my high school physics class and got an A on the final test. So, I think I can confidently approach this from a scientific point of view to prove the evidence confirms the events at the hotel are paranormal."

"Okay, you've got my attention," Kat said, interested in where her sister's argument was going.

"Science tells us that human beings are nothing more than a collection of energy guided by the brain," Nicole said, laying the foundation for her idea.

Mariah, who'd failed her senior physics class and had had to retake the course, said, "I'm a little rusty on my science, but, as I remember, Einstein stated that energy cannot be created or destroyed; it can only change forms. So, when we die, when the energy is no longer needed to operate the electrical system of our bodies, where does it go?"

Nicole tried to explain, "I believe a person's life energy—or soul—passes to Heaven upon death. But when the life energy is released from someone who'd once had a strong connection to the property, the hotel sucks it up like a vacuum cleaner. Trapped, unable to move on, the energy stays behind, retaining the form it'd held in life. These earthbound spirits do not understand what has happened to them. Caught in limbo, unaware of their own passing, the spirits re-live the past over-and-over again. If the energy left behind is strong enough, the spirit is able to move objects, and their voice or image can be recorded."

Kat shook her head at such a ridiculous thought. "You've got to be joking. You really want us to believe that the hotel is some sort of giant paranormal vacuum cleaner, sucking the souls out of the dead?"

"Think about it," Nicole demanded. "The Crescent Mountain, the hilltop the hotel sits on, is predominantly limestone. This is the very same stone used for the body of the hotel. There has always been a sweeping assumption among paranormal investigators that this type of rock has the ability to absorb and release energy."

Mariah considered Nicole's idea for a moment, then turned to Kat for her opinion. "If Nicole is correct, when someone dies, their life energy gets absorbed and sometimes presents itself to guests in the form of a ghost. Is this paranormal or scientific proof that the hotel is haunted?"

Kat shook her head. "It's neither." She looked at her sister and explained, "The 'A' in science only means you passed the semester's multiple-choice test. Obviously, you did not have a true understanding of the law of energy."

Nicole had to restrain the impulse to punch her sister. She hated the superior attitude Kat so often took when talking about science. "Okay, Einstein, what's the science?"

"The answer is very simple and not at all mysterious. Humans and other organisms *do* generate very low-level electrical currents; these currents are no longer produced once the organism dies. Because the source of energy stops, the electrical current stops—just as a light bulb turns off when you switch off the electricity running to it. So, there is absolutely no chance that a person's *soul*

could magically get sucked up and trans-
formed into a spooky form of energy."
Rubbing a kink at the back of her neck, Kat
scolded Nicole for her wrongheaded thinking.
"Neither Einstein nor his laws of physics
suggest hauntings are real. Paranormal
investigators who repeat the claim that the
laws of energy provide a sound basis for the
existence of life after death reveal less about
ghosts than they do about their poor
understanding of basic science."

"Please, enlighten us then," Nicole
demanded. "What's your explanation for all
the ghostly activity?"

Brows wrinkled in deep thought, Kat
quickly pieced together her defense. "There
are several factors that contribute to the
reports of unusual activities at the hotel. The
first requirement for seeing ghosts is believing
there *are* ghosts. Guests immediately attribute
anything unusual as paranormal because of
the hotel's haunted reputation, and because
they come here wanting to experience the
supernatural." Giving her sister credit, she
said, "You were right about energy having
something to do with the seemingly spooky
events at the hotel. Limestone *does* have a
special ability, but it's not that it can absorb

someone's soul upon death, but that it can transmit electromagnetic energy. As seen on the paranormal reality TV shows you are so fond of watching, ghost hunters use electronic devices like night vision cameras and EMF meters, which measure and record electro-magnetic energy. This is not proof of ghosts, but of electronic activity near the device."

Not convinced, Nicole cut in, "Then what accounts for unusual noises, such as the clawing sounds we heard or footsteps on the stairs or in the halls?"

Kat had an answer. "The Crescent Hotel has sat on this mountaintop for over a century. It's only natural that the floors creak, doors squeak, and the plumbing rattles."

"That's an asinine explanation," Nicole argued, shaking her head at such a stupid idea.

Frustrated, Kat shot back, "No more ridiculous than the paranormal assumptions you touted as scientific facts. Don't you get it? Ghost hunters are manipulating your mind by selling you something that is not in line with the basic laws of physics. The entire ghost-hunting business, just like Baker and his cancer cure, is based on fake science, and none of these so-called investigators you hold in such high regard should be taken seriously."

Kat and Nicole glared daggers at each other from across the room. It didn't take an Einstein genius to figure out that both sides were dug in, neither willing to give an inch in the ghost wars.

Mariah also knew they would turn on her if she even *hinted* at taking sides. Like a negotiator in a hostage situation, she had to tread likely, so she took the only course of action left. "There are only two possible conclusions. The first is that ghosts exist, and the hotel is haunted. The second option is ghosts do *not* exist, and the hotel is *not* haunted."

Mariah scanned the faces of her two friends and waited. Using her hair like a security blanket, she fidgeted with the long braid draped across her chest. Negotiations at a standstill, she needed to broker a truce without revealing she had been harassed by the spirits of the hotel from the first moment she had stepped into the lobby.

Finally, Kat and Nicole nodded, and Mariah continued, "In the end, it doesn't matter what all the scientists, skeptics, or paranormal investigators think. If ghosts are real, their existence will be discovered and verified by scientists through controlled experiments sooner or later, not by weekend ghost-hunters wandering around the Crescent Hotel late at night with cameras and EFM devices. Therefore, my recommendation is that the inexplicable occurrences at the hotel warrant further scientific investigation by our newly formed team of ghost detectives."

"What?" Kat yelled, finding it hard to believe what she had just heard.

Nicole was as surprised as her sister by Mariah's conclusion. "After all our evidence, this is the best you could come up with? Book another spooky vacation at the most haunted hotel in America?"

"Let's face the facts. For the two of you, ghost-hunting is not really about finding the evidence," Mariah defended her stance. "If it were, the search would have been abandoned days ago. Instead, it's all about having fun with friends, hearing spooky tales, and searching around the edge of the unknown for answers to questions that have no answers."

Gently, shoving aside the invisible tabby cat brushing up against her leg, Mariah stood and announced, "After all, everyone loves a good ghost story."

# Epilogue

**The** limestone castle sat below the blue moon, shrouded in a sea of mist. The glorious structure had reigned atop the mountain for over a century. Proud, majestic, the crowning glory of the picturesque Victorian village below, there was no reason to believe it would not rule for another hundred.

The rumors, questions, and suspicions that had always swirled around the stone fortress lured a steady stream of inquisitive visitors to its location. Over the years, many convinced themselves there was something special about this place that made visitors imagine the halls and rooms were inhabited with spirits from beyond the grave. Many believed the unusual activity within its walls must be studied, verified, and documented for future generations.

In the embrace of darkening shadows, it breathed deep and long. The jewel of the

Ozarks had put on quite the song-and-dance for the most recent round of curiosity seekers. They would return. They always did. This time, those who possessed the courage *just* might find in the dark what had eluded them in the light.

# Acknowledgments

We would like to express our appreciation to several people; without their support and encouragement, this book would not have been written.

A special thanks goes to Resort Hostess Niki Emerson of the 1886 Crescent Hotel and Spa. Even with her busy schedule, she was willing to take time to answer questions and offer helpful suggestions.

Our deepest gratitude to Sean-Paul and Juliane Fay of Intrigue Theater for taking an interest in our book and giving us helpful advice and recommendations. A visit to your theater is always the highlight of our trips to Eureka Springs.

Sincere thanks to Lisa, owner of Oracle & Sage, for the very helpful suggestions. We never miss a chance to stop in and shop when visiting the Victorian town of Eureka Springs.

We are very grateful to Terry Blanton, owner of the New Orleans Hotel, for permission to showcase the Voodoo Lounge in a chapter of our book. When in Eureka Springs, we always make time for one of the hotel's signature cocktails.

Thank you to Jeff Danos, Director of Operations of the Eureka Springs Historical Museum, for his invaluable assistance with our research of Norman Baker and the cancer clinic. We are also thankful to the museum board for permitting us to use the 1886 photograph of the Crescent Hotel and for their willingness to preview our book.

We would like to recognize Jerri Marlowe, the 1905 Basin Park Hotel Resort Hostess. Jerri has always been generous with her time and willingness to share her knowledge of the history of Eureka Springs. We appreciate her suggestions and insights.

A huge thank you to Benny Clark, the real-life inspiration for our fictional character, Benny the Crescent Hotel's courtesy van driver.

A big shoutout to Kathy Ann Rhoden for so graciously sharing information about her family, the Gideon Bible, and her parents' connection to the history of the 1886 Cresent Hotel and Spa.

To our family and friends, we appreciate your never-ending encouragement and support, even though you do not share our fascination for spirits who reside on the "dark side."

# Books by CC Brown

## Ghosts of Perry House

Ghosts walk the halls and haunt the rooms of the 1905 Basin Park Hotel, one of Arkansas' most famous vacation destinations. A late-night guided tour of the historical hotel reveals guests repeatedly report sightings of the ghostly figure of a cowboy in a white canvas duster with a six-shooter strapped to his hip prowling the halls of the third floor. Determined to discover an explanation for the unexplainable, Nicole, her sister, and their longtime friend launch an investigation into the dark history of the hotel. The trio soon becomes entangled in a century-old mystery filled with ghosts, hauntings, and terrifying secrets.

## Black Widow Society

The sacred relic of the undead, the *Vampire Bible* has fallen into the hands of paranormal-artifact dealer, Koleen O'Brien. An eBay bid and an annual vacation lead Koleen and her friends to San Antonio to deliver the book to a wealthy Texan. They are clueless to the fact that a pack of blood-thirsty vampires is stalking them to reclaim the Bible. Immortals meet their match as they discover that these women aren't typical mortals, they're members of the Black Widow Society!

## Wolf Stone

Just when Dmitri thought nothing could stop him from executing his plan to become king of the shapeshifters sexy Mona Dix enters the scene. The sacred relic of the werewolf nation, the Wolf Stone, has fallen into her hands. With the possession of the stone comes the power to dominate and rule the thirteen werewolf tribes.

Vacationing on the Oregon coast in the rugged terrain of the redwood forest, Mona and her friends are unaware of Dmitri and the pack of ancient wolves in hot pursuit to retrieve their precious stone. For the first time, Dmitri meets a woman who is more than a match for his supernatural powers and strong will. She is a Black Widow and a member of the "Society."

# Ghosts of Perry House
Available at Amazon.com

# Chapter 1
## Present

**Black** clouds blotted out the setting sun as the Moneyland tour bus navigated the serpentine road leading to Eureka Springs, Arkansas. Ancient oaks lined the bluffs, forming a naturally arched tunnel. Trees commanded by the powerful winds lost hold of their leaves. Snapped limbs whirled through the air, littering the roadway. Caught in nature's wrath, the bus driver, unfamiliar with the route, death-gripped the wheel and prayed for a place to pull over.

Prayers unanswered and trapped in a stormy nightmare, he fought to keep the bus on the highway as he slowed to descend the dangerously steep grade.

"Bingo!" echoed up and down the dimly lit aisle and ricocheted off bus windows. The five-letter word brought a chorus of good-natured moans and groans from the losers.

The winner screamed her excitement and waved the lucky card.

A strong gust of wind rocked the bus. The bingo official staggered to the back to confirm the numbers. Fighting to stay upright, she accidentally bumped Nicole's elbow, sending her paranormal romance to the floor.

"What the…?" Nicole grumbled, retrieving her new, but now scuffed, paperback. She tossed the book to Kat, her sister, then stood, turned, and knelt in the seat, peering over the headrest. The silhouettes were vigorously fanning themselves with their worthless cards. It was obvious that the air-conditioning system couldn't crank out enough cool air to keep up with the extreme July heat.

Lightning flicked repeatedly like a reporter's camera at the premiere of a much-anticipated horror movie. In that violent illumination, Nicole saw concern growing in the eyes and actions of the other tourists. Some, visibly shaken by the severity of the storm, stared, wide-eyed, bracing them-selves for the next round. Others chattered nervously about no cell phone reception, while a few, unconcerned with the weather, cleared their pull-down tables, anticipating the next bingo game. Her friend, Mariah, in the row directly behind, fell into the last category.

"Let the good times roll!" Mariah yelled, reveling in the chaos and excitement, impatiently swiping at the dark threads of unruly hair tickling her face.

Again, lightning flashed, and passengers shrieked. Nicole heard Kat counting, "One-Mississippi, two-Mississippi, three-Mississippi," a method she always used to gauge the closeness of a storm. Then the thunder cracked. A quick mental calculation told Kat the strike was close. She looked at Nicole. "That was less than a mile."

Finding everyone's reaction, including Kat's, overly theatrical and verging on hyster-ical, Nicole hollered, "People, it's just a thunderstorm!" Disgusted, she plopped back into her seat and gathered sticky blonde strands, then pulled them through a hair tie from her wrist. "What in the world were you thinking?" she demanded, as she whirled in her seat, the soggy ponytail lashed her sister in the face…

"Ouch!" Kat yelped, grabbing her stinging cheek. "Actually, right now, I'm thinking about snatching you, bald-headed," she ground out between clenched teeth.

Realizing what she had done, Nicole quickly came back with, "I'd like to say I'm sorry, but I'm not. You deserved that and more." Her sapphire-blue eyes shot daggers.

Blinking green eyes, feigning innocence, Kat mockingly smoothed her sleek, chin-length, auburn bob before answering, "Hey, I have no control over the weather or AC. My hair loves the heat and humidity."

"Cut the crap, Katherine Lynette." Nicole resorted to using Kat's full name to emphasize her annoyance. "You know perfectly well what I'm talking about. I told you this morning there was a storm alert for Northern Arkansas and didn't want to take the bus. Did you listen? Hell, no." She stopped the rant as it reached a crescendo.

Kat hated it when her sister used her given name. "Brother, you're impossible to please!" Kat shot back, fidgeting with her designer, black-framed glasses as they slid down her nose. Pushing them back in place, she explained, "I saw the ad for the travel agency while cruising the Internet that said, 'Take the bus, earn a few bucks, and leave the driving to us.' It seemed a perfect fit for our weekend retreat: for dollars, for spa treatments, for sightseeing—"

Kat's explanation was interrupted by an explosion of forked, blue-white lightning as it struck the bus. A blast like a sonic boom shook the earth. The interior lights flipped off and on, and then… complete darkness.

Startled, some folks cried out in terror; others loudly voiced their opinion of Moneyland Tours and their driver.

Right on cue, the rain fell. It came in torrents, hammering the windows, splattering the pavement, and silencing the protests. The swoosh of wipers and the hiss of tires were amplified. The substantial rains, driven by the wind, caused the bus to hydroplane. The rear end began to veer to the left, crossing the double-yellow center line. Cries of alarm were muffled by the kettledrum rumble overhead.

Panicking, the driver jerked the wheel, sending bingo cards flying and launching one startled passenger from his seat.

"Slow down!" someone yelled.

"Help! He's trying to kill us!" a silver-headed senior squawked in distress.

*My life's in the hands of an idiot!* Kat warned herself.

An older man, immediately to her right, jumped to his feet and roared, "Steer into the skid!" The authoritative voice drowned out other instructions being hurled at the driver.

With trembling hands, the driver steered left-to-right and then right-to-left, finally regaining control of the bus. Shaken and trying desperately to regroup, he tackled the unruly mob. "Sit down and shut up!" he bellowed. "We're not off this mountain yet!" The bus inched a path around storm debris and continued its journey to the valley below.

Kat, relieved to see the driver was back in command and the storm was losing steam, relaxed her death grip on the armrest. *Maybe I'm not going to die today.*

She turned away from her sister's accusing eyes to watch raindrops splash against the windowpane. She refused to continue defending her choice of transportation. Recently, dealing with Nicole was like trying to navigate a minefield; if she didn't watch her step, the results could be explosive. The death of Nicole's two-year-old son had been such an unusual and unexpected event; a simple cold had spiraled out of control and turned deadly. The consequences of the loss eventually led to emotional estrangement, apathy, and indifference toward her marriage. Ultimately, divorce had been the only solution. Kat knew Nicole would never get over the loss of her son, but it was time for her to let go of the grief. No way was she going to give her sister the opportunity to back out on the trip. Nicole needed to move on and rebuild her life.

Nicole said nothing, but she'd glimpsed something in Kat's eyes just before she turned away, and she didn't like it, not one bit. The look of concern mingled with something else… pity.

Angry, she decided to ignore her sister. Listening to the tempo of the wipers, she kicked off her leather flip-flops and settled back into the cushiony seat.

Mariah picked up on the negative vibes coming from the sisters. The sibling squabble sucked every last particle of positive energy out of the air like a black hole attracting light to its darkness. She had learned not to intervene in a conflict between the two. It was a no-win situation for the referee. Staying neutral while identifying the villain and the victim of the conflict never turned out well for her. One of the two always retaliated by turning her ire on Mariah.

Her thoughts were interrupted as she caught a slight whiff of something. It floated on the air briefly, but then, was gone. She recognized the woody, sweet-like aroma of newly crushed tobacco. Her grandfather always kept a tin of pipe tobacco sitting near his rocker. The same tart, deep cherry scent would ease into every room when he smoked.

*Is some idiot really smoking?* She looked around. None of the passengers had a guilty face. *Strange, smoking on buses and planes had been banned for years.* Giving up on finding the offender, she turned and stared out into the rain-streaked night. There was an ominous feel to the lengthening shadows of the misshapen and twisted trees lining the road.

*O-o-oh, Lord!* Mariah shuddered in response to a sudden shiver. "Someone just walked over the ground that shall be my grave." She quoted an old wives' tale she had heard as a child, a superstition that foretold the approach of trouble.

Reaching into her jeans pocket, she dug for the buckeye. The power of the odd-shaped, brown nut wasn't scientific. Just like a rabbit's foot, horseshoe, or four-leaf clover, the buckeye had its doubters. However, it was oddly comforting to roll the talisman between her fingers.

Made in the USA
Monee, IL
28 September 2023

43595302R00148